Courtney James spre **towel on a tiny, priva** **shore of Green Bay.** She stretched out face down and loosened the clasp of her strapless bikini bra to let the sun warm every exposed inch. After a moment relaxing to the water's quiet lapping, she turned over, forearm flung up to shade her eyes. Her full, rose-tipped breasts thrust toward the sun, accepting its warmth but longing for the touch that would never thrill her again.

Would she ever forget? It had been almost two years since her husband's fatal NASCAR accident. "Ronnie—" she murmured, reaching out to catch his memory and encountering instead a handful of unfamiliar cloth. Her eyes flew open. "Oh!"

A formidably tall and solid silhouette loomed above her, dark against the afternoon sun. She blinked and squinted, clutching the material.

"I'm not Ronnie," said the silhouette's low, resonant voice. "But I wish I were." There was a hint of laughter behind his words.

Heart pounding, Courtney sat up, clutching the man's shirt that had been softly laid across her body. She caught her breath. There probably wasn't a living soul anywhere within shouting distance.

As her eyes adjusted to the afternoon glare, her mind unconsciously catalogued the man standing widespread above her, and an unexpected flush flooded her whole body. His skin had a gingery tinge. Dark hair, shining wet, waved thickly above heavy brows that nearly met over his nose. His jaw line was firm, as was the rest of his well-muscled body.

Wide-eyed, a little frightened, flustered and embarrassed as well, Courtney indignantly scrambled to her feet. She fumbled in the sand for her elusive bra with one hand and clutched his shirt with the other while keeping her eyes warily on the man.

The Door to Love

by

Nancy Sweetland

The Door to Love

Cover Art by *Angela Anderson*

The Wild Rose Press
PO Box 708
Adams Basin, NY 14410-0706
Visit us at www.thewildrosepress.com

Publishing History
First Champagne Rose Edition, 2009
Print ISBN 1-60154-472-3

Published in the United States of America

Dedication

For Bob Sweetland, who believed in love, and in me.

Chapter One

Courtney James spread her colorful beach towel on a tiny, private sunning spot on the shore of Green Bay. She stretched out face down and loosened the clasp of her strapless bikini bra to let the sun warm every exposed inch. After a moment relaxing to the water's quiet lapping, she turned over, forearm flung up to shade her eyes. Her full, rose-tipped breasts thrust toward the sun, accepting its warmth but longing for the touch that would never thrill her again.

Would she ever forget? It had been almost two years since her husband's fatal NASCAR accident. "Ronnie—" she murmured, reaching out to catch his memory and encountering instead a handful of unfamiliar cloth. Her eyes flew open. "Oh!"

A formidably tall and solid silhouette loomed above her, dark against the afternoon sun. She blinked and squinted, clutching the material.

"I'm not Ronnie," said the silhouette's low, resonant voice. "But I wish I were." There was a hint of laughter behind his words.

Heart pounding, Courtney sat up, clutching the man's shirt that had been softly laid across her body. She caught her breath. There probably wasn't a living soul anywhere within shouting distance.

As her eyes adjusted to the afternoon glare, her mind unconsciously catalogued the man standing widespread above her, and an unexpected flush flooded her whole body. His skin had a gingery tinge. Dark hair, shining wet, waved thickly above heavy brows that nearly met over his nose. His jaw line

1

was firm, as was the rest of his well-muscled body.

Wide-eyed, a little frightened, flustered and embarrassed as well, Courtney indignantly scrambled to her feet. She fumbled in the sand for her elusive bra with one hand and clutched his shirt with the other while keeping her eyes warily on the man. Even in her confusion she was fully aware that whoever he was, he was one of the most virile, physically attractive men she had ever met. His body, clad only in brief black swim trunks was the picture of health and vitality. Tiny water prisms sparkled in the dark hair on his chest and ran in droplets down his muscled abs toward his low-slung suit.

Smoky grey eyes studied hers. "I trust you don't mind me lending my shirt." His voice still carried that annoying hint of laughter. "I'd been swimming for some time, and I thought you were getting burnt. Especially on..." he paused and raised level, dark brows, "some particular parts of your lovely body."

"Oh!" Courtney said again, backing away, nearly stumbling as one bare foot caught in her beach towel. Her long hair fell across his firm, muscled arm as he caught her shoulder to steady her.

"Easy, there." He gently let go. "You're not quite awake."

She rubbed her shoulder where her skin tingled from his touch, aware that the laughter hadn't left his eyes. Where was that bra, anyway? Irritated at being in such an embarrassing situation, she stared up at him, eyes widening at the unreadable expression in his. "Wh-what are you doing here!" she demanded.

"That might be my question to you," he said. "And don't look so frightened. I don't eat little girls, even honey-colored ones." He reached down, whipped back the corner of her towel and dangled a wisp of red material. "Looking for this?" His deep voice still carried that amusement and caused another unwelcome flush through her body.

"Yes, thank you. And I'll thank you as well to turn around while I put it on." She snatched the bra.

"Yes, Ma'am," he said, but he didn't turn away. "And then perhaps you'll tell me what you're doing trespassing on my property."

"*Your* property!" Courtney's eyes widened again. Another masterful male. Her world seemed peopled with them. Even Ronnie had shown chauvinistic tendencies at times, as had his friend Jerry. And there was Logan Andrews, who felt it his duty to advise her both in and out of the workplace. Well, she'd soon set *this* one straight. She was well within her rights, and as soon as she was decently clad she'd tell him so, whoever he was.

Courtney stared stone-faced at the man for a few seconds. His expression didn't change except for a quizzical tilt of his head and a slight raise of his dark brows. She gave in, turned her back to him and tucked her breasts into the bra, fumbling behind for the clasp that entangled with the curly ends of her long hair. "Damn!"

"Here, let me," he said, still exhibiting that tinge of underlying humor. "I know a little bit about those things."

Before she could step away, but not before her body responded alarmingly, he quickly manipulated the clasp. Most likely he'd had a good deal of practice with bra hooks.

She reached down for her towel and shook the sand from it with a couple of furious snaps. She draped it around her shoulders, pulled her heavy hair from under it and met his gaze with her chin thrust out.

"Don't cover up," he said. "You're very beautiful, you know. I won't bite, really, and the sun is magnificent. Don't you feel it?"

His smoky gaze enveloped her.

What she felt was not the sun. For the first time since Ronnie James's death, Courtney felt alive.

Chapter Two

Courtney snugged the beach towel tightly across her slim shoulders, feeling the strength of his penetrating gaze even though she now wore both pieces of her swimsuit. "Who are you?" she demanded, narrowing her eyes. "And what are you doing on my beach?"

"Correction. *My* beach. I'm Lincoln Spencer. Link to my friends—one of whom I hope you might come to be. And I happen to own this little stretch of sand you're so comfortably sunning on."

"But Amy Lane owned it—oh!" Of course. Remembering Amy's death brought understanding. "You must be the prodigal nephew I heard so much about. The Great Chicago Lawyer, capital G.C.L., according to Amy." Courtney wrinkled her nose. "And you've inherited her property and have come to kick me off, have you? Melodrama! Successful lawyer heir displaces hard-working girl, etcetera, etcetera! Well, just try it!" She tossed her head, chin up, light fronds of her blond hair forming a halo around her head. "I've got a contract, you know!"

"Have you now?" That light, laughing-at-her tone was back in his voice. "And did Amy also tell you that I'm really an ogre in disguise, or have you figured that part out for yourself?" His eyes smoldered and a muscle twitched alongside his square jaw. "I'd guess that being rude is hardly part of your normal personality. Or is it?"

How she hated condescension...but did he really own the property? Careful, Courtney, she told herself, you can't afford to get off on the wrong foot with Mr. Big.

She dropped her gaze but quickly looked up again as that unwelcome warmth surged through her body at the sight of his well-proportioned physique. What in the world was wrong with her that she would react so physically to a complete stranger, and be rude as well?

"I am sorry. Shall we start again?" She held out her right hand to shake his, still clutching the towel with her left. "Thanks for the shirt, and the concern. You startled me, and I guess I put up my defenses. I'm Courtney James, and I'm buying the building and the cottage from Amy Lane. I'm not used to anyone coming here."

The man's brows nearly met as he stepped toward her, frowning. "You're buying what?"

She involuntarily moved back at his scowl. Was he deaf? "The store and the cottage, I said." She pointed toward the wooden building that stood on the waterfront a half-block down the shore and the small, pine-green cottage above and behind it. "You didn't know?"

His grey eyes narrowed. "I most certainly did not. I've handled Amy's affairs for years and she never mentioned anything about any such contract. I presume you have some documents to prove your claim?"

"Claim!" Courtney gasped.

"You wouldn't be the first to take advantage of a senile old woman." His eyes were darker now, and not friendly.

"Senile!" Courtney parroted his word. "Amy was no more senile than you are!" she sputtered. "And she was certainly a darn sight nicer!" Then, remembering long, cozy talks in front of Amy's crackling fire, Courtney choked up. "We were good friends, and since she died it's been desolate here."

Courtney caught her breath and almost whispered, "I miss her dreadfully."

He softened visibly, and his cold, businesslike voice warmed. "I'm sorry. I do, too. She was both my mother and my father for most of my life." He picked up his shirt that Courtney had dropped on the sand, shook it out, and pulled it over his head. He still didn't smile, but he seemed more human and less like a marble Greek god. Courtney felt her shoulders relax a little.

He spoke as he straightened his collar. "Sorry if I offended you, but this comes as a complete surprise. I had plans to use the building as a fishing tackle and ski rental. In fact, I'm here to talk with the man I've lined up to run it. It's something I've wanted to do ever since Tom died. Amy and I talked about it often."

"B-but that's what I'm doing! I'm opening next week along with the Blossom Time!" Her puzzled eyes searched his. "Why would she have agreed, if you—? In fact, she suggested the idea to me!"

"I can't answer that. But at least I know you aren't a trespasser. That's something." He smiled, finally, changing his whole appearance to handsomely appealing. "Am I forgiven?"

Courtney smiled back, reluctantly. "Of course. Now I'd better get back to work." She paused. "Can we be friends?"

He stared into her eyes for a long, disturbing moment before he grinned. "Friends," he said, nodding. "I don't see why not."

But as he followed her up the rugged pine-shadowed rugged path toward their twin cottages, she heard him add softly, "For now."

****

Friends, thought Courtney, as she unpacked the last carton of brilliant red and white Daredevil lures. *For now*? What had he meant by that? Maybe he was planning to see that her agreement with Amy Lane didn't hold?

Friends. Those that she had were miles away now. She gathered empty packing cases and swept up elusive Styrofoam popcorns. Sister Bay people were welcoming, but she simply hadn't made much effort to meet them, being so busy first planning, then working to get her store in order. She had to be ready for the official Grand Opening of Courtney's Sports, her first independent venture into the business world. She hoped for an onslaught of tourists for Blossom Time. The annual festival celebrating Door County's cheerfully blooming cherry orchards might very well determine the success or failure of her business.

Courtney wasn't going to think about failure. She winced, slowly rotated her sore shoulders and lifted her heavy hair away from the moist warmth of her neck. Sweltering in May's unseasonable heat, Courtney had spent all yesterday and the cooler hours of this morning ripping open boxes, deciding on displays, shelving and pricing equipment purchased with most of Ronnie's insurance money. The rest had gone for a down payment on the shoreline cottage and store. And now what? What if she lost it all to the great G.C.L.? What then?

Her face flushed as she thought of the scene on the shore. What was Link Spencer like, really? Attractive, certainly. Way too sure of himself. Successful, too, according to Amy, who'd doted on him and his burgeoning practice. Courtney shook her head. Why would a Chicago lawyer want to own a fishing tackle shop? And if Amy knew he was even thinking about it, why, oh why had she encouraged Courtney to go into the store?

Courtney tried to recall more about Lincoln Spencer from Amy's conversations. Why hadn't he married? Something about being too wrapped up in law and his political aspirations to have much time left over for women. Courtney hadn't really listened; her loss of Ronnie had been too raw for her to force an interest in any man.

She stubbed the broom into the corner behind an open carton of puffy orange life jackets. "There! And I quit. That's enough for today." Thumbs hooked into the pockets of her denim jeans, she surveyed the showroom. Not big, but shelved efficiently and stocked well enough for any ordinary fisherman. After all, they weren't going to be angling for barracuda or swordfish here. Her customers would be just the ordinary tourist after that elusive "bigger-than-usual-anything-that-would-bite," was the way Amy had put it.

"Stock what families need to take their kids on the water, first of all," she'd advised. "That's what my Tom did when he ran the tackle store. It was a success, too." She'd smiled, remembering, a soft look of past happiness on Amy's lined face. Tom Lane had been Amy's beloved husband for over fifty years. "Don't think I don't know how lonely you're feeling," She had patted Courtney's arm. "I thought my life ended when Tom was gone." Her faded eyes misted. "But it didn't, and yours won't either. So put that store together. Busy yourself with it and make it go. Heaven knows we've needed one on this end of town ever since Tom died, and I think you've got the spunk to make it work."

Spunk. That was a better attribute than rudeness. Courtney made a face, remembering Lincoln Spencer's remark. If she weren't careful she'd be out on her ear, lock, stock and the proverbial barrel.

"And that wouldn't be funny," she said, then smiled. Being alone so much she'd begun talking to herself. "It's a good thing Lisbet's coming for the summer and bringing Andy. He can use some sunshine and good times." The last few rough years had ended in her sister Lisbet's rotten divorce.

She wondered if there was any other kind, reliving the bitter custody fight over seven-year-old Andy. The sympathetic judge finally awarded the boy to his mother, but psychological damage took its toll and Andy, asthmatic and physically slight, had suffered from a number of ailments over the past winter. It would be good for him to spend time outdoors, and to get him away from Lisbet's hovering for even a few hours a day.

The rasp of a cleared throat startled Courtney from her thoughts.

"Sorry. I've been standing here for five minutes, and your woolgathering was so intense you didn't hear me. I do seem to surprise you more than I intend." Lincoln Spencer's tall frame at the door was now clad in white tailored shorts and a navy shirt, open at the throat, a combination casually enhancing his dark good looks. "May I come in?"

Courtney collected her thoughts. And her manners. "Certainly. The store is open, just not officially as yet. That happens next week."

He looked around the packed shelves. "Nice layout. Attractive. Looks a little more organized than my Uncle Tom's was, as I remember. Could use a bit more clothing; there's room for a couple of racks."

Courtney bristled at his advice but said nothing. She hoped to add sports attire when she could swing the cost.

He walked around the store. "What are you going to do to catch the hotel trade? Those places are pretty much at the other end of the bay."

Darn! Why did he have to hit on the one thing that bothered her about her location? "True. But there are quite a few cottages nearby where families stay. And I'll advertise. I've got posters all over the guesthouses. Word of mouth should help."

"Yes. Well, we certainly want to make a go of this, don't we?"

"We!" Courtney's eyes widened. "What do you mean, we?"

That infuriating look was back in his grey eyes, along with the light tone of voice. "Didn't you read your contract? I've been going over the one Amy left in her desk. It seems I own a half interest in Courtney's Sports until you've satisfied the complete down payment."

"Oh!" Courtney stepped backwards, her mouth open, her thoughts swirling. Of course. She'd needed working capital, and what she'd given Amy from Ronnie's insurance money hadn't been enough for the required down payment. She was to fulfill the whole amount with part of her monthly profits. It hadn't occurred to Courtney that the same arrangement would transfer to the heir of the property. Lincoln Spencer, to be exact. The G.L.C.

She felt a flush of embarrassment. "I didn't realize—"

He chuckled as he picked up a rod and reel and looked it over, testing the drag. "Most women wouldn't."

Her chin came up. "Most women wouldn't what?"

"Realize much about legalities. Didn't you know what you signed?"

"Of course I did!" she snapped, thrusting out her chin. "I just didn't expect Amy to die and turn me over to the likes of you!" Something—anger? sorrow?—flickered in his eyes. She took a deep breath. "Well, then. I'll just have to buy you out, and that will solve both our problems, won't it?" Her mind raced and even as she spoke she felt her stomach crawl. Where could she get the money? She'd put every spare cent she had into stocking the store.

"Oh, no," he said, strolling down an aisle and surveying the showroom more thoroughly. He tested the sharpness of a filleting knife blade against his thumb. "I don't want to sell. You're doing what I wanted to do with the building—though I probably would have done it differently."

She just bet he would. Biting her lip, she held back a retort and restrained herself from trying to physically throw him out.

She watched as he ran his finger along the edge of a counter holding sinkers and swivels. "I think I like owning part of Courtney's Sports. And that gives me the right to pop in now and then, doesn't it?" He smiled cheerfully at her.

If he thought he would get a pleasant reaction to that, he would be disappointed. "Well, you can just pop out. I don't need any advice on how to run my business, thank you. Now, I've got a lot of work to do, and standing around here talking isn't getting it done." Courtney abruptly turned her back to him, walked into the stockroom and slammed the door behind her.

Leaning against the rough wooden doorframe, she held back tears. What an inexperienced fool she was, and how stupid she must look to Amy's Great Chicago Lawyer.

Humiliation—and frustration—twice in one day from the same impossible man. She balled her hands into fists, took a deep breath and let it out slowly, mentally counting to fifteen. Ten wasn't enough.

Surely he wouldn't stay long at Amy's other cottage only yards from hers, poking his well-shaped nose into her business and telling her how to run it. Surely, she hoped, a successful city lawyer like Mr. Lincoln Spencer would have too many cases and be too involved in city life to spend much time around a sleepy little town like Sister Bay.

Chapter Three

Courtney busied herself counting packets of fishhooks in the stock room until she was sure Lincoln Spencer had left, then opened the door cautiously and peered through the crack. No one in sight.

Relieved, she picked up an open carton of round red and white plastic bobbers, stepped through the door into the display area and nearly dropped the whole rattling gross of floats when a peevish high-pitched voice complained, "Well, finally! I thought nobody was here! Someone could steal you blind, you know? That is, if anybody *wanted* this stuff."

Courtney whirled around to face a petite bleached blond wearing unbelievably brief white shorts and a skimpy blue star-patterned bandanna over ample breasts. She carried the ultimate in a matching flowered sun hat. Her petite figure was picture perfect but at the same time voluptuous. Her attitude toward Courtney was that of addressing a servant—and a most unimportant one, at that.

Swallowing instant dislike, Courtney waited just a moment before answering. If this was an example of the summer clientele she was going to have, she'd better learn to be pleasant. But it wouldn't be easy. She smiled. "Sorry, I was in the stockroom. May I help you with something?"

The blond's heavily shadowed, mascara-darkened blue eyes widened into black-fringed circles above brilliant red lips. "Good heavens, no!" she said, shaking back her short curly mane. "I'm no fisherperson, for God's sake. I just need directions. I'm looking for Lincoln Spencer, and at the hotel they said he was somewhere around here. I don't suppose *you'd* know where, would you?"

Her manner implied that Courtney wasn't nearly sophisticated enough to be acquainted with any such person. Courtney hid a smile as she wondered what the oh-so-condescending blond would think about the bare realities of Courtney's shore meeting with the imposing Mr. Spencer. She bent down to place the box of bobbers on the pine-planked floor.

"Oh, you mean Link?" she said innocently. "Of course, I surely do know him—he was here just a minute ago, but as I didn't have time to chat, he left. You'll probably find him at the brown cottage up the hill." Courtney pointed toward the wooded path that skirted the store and ran up the incline between the two cabins. "Or down at the water. Is he expecting you?"

The blond raised her carefully plucked and darkened eyebrows. "Well, he'd better be!" She turned on her sandaled high heels and strutted out the door, tossing back over her shoulder, "He'd just better be!"

Courtney watched the flash of white legs as the woman hurried up the shady, pine-needled path toward Amy's second cottage, her stiletto heels sinking into the ground with every step. "She could have said *thanks* or *go to hell* or something," Courtney muttered. And then came the familiar wretch of loneliness. Though the blond didn't seem the type Courtney would have thought appealing to Lincoln Spencer, at least he wouldn't spend the next few hours—or more, who knew?—alone. "Oh, Ronnie," she breathed. Would her loss ever be easier to bear? Had she been right to come here to forget?

"You're making a mistake, Court," Logan

Andrews, her boss at Ladd's Milwaukee department store had declared. "Door County's great—in the summer. Like a little piece of New England transplanted here in the Midwest, with all its harbors and sailboats and crazy tourists. But what about after the season? What about your interest in theater? The cultural aspects you've enjoyed here? With me? Besides—" He had fingered his elegant gold watch fob as he grinned engagingly and gave her one of his flirtatious winks. "I'll miss you."

Courtney smiled, remembering her answer. "You'll survive, I'm sure of that."

She returned to her tasks and finished hanging large, colorful lures on the pegboard wall behind one showcase, where their brilliant enameled hues brightened the whole area. She didn't yet know what most of them were supposed to catch, but a few more nights of study would help. There wasn't much else to do in the evenings anyway.

Courtney leaned against the edge of the open door and looked up at the darkening western sky. Only a ribbon of brilliant orange marked day's end across the bay's quiet water where one small sailboat moving quietly toward shore was a dark triangle against the colorful backdrop. Children's shouts echoed up the shore as lights began to glow, one by one, in the cooling evening air.

This was the time of day Courtney dreaded most, when husbands came home to their families and everyone settled in for the evening. It was the part of day that she most wished she and Ronnie had had a child.

"Not yet, Courtney. There's time." Ronnie kept putting her off, not ready to stop being the child himself. Then, suddenly, in a screech of rubber and flash of fire, it was too late.

"Quit feeling sorry for yourself," Courtney said. She closed the store door with a snap and walked slowly up the hill to where the path branched and stopped to look once more across the bay. The orange light had faded now; only a dusky mauve spread above the water. The little sailboat had gone home. She sighed unconsciously and turned left toward her empty cottage.

Tomorrow Lisbet and Andy would arrive and they would make all the difference—she was alone too much. And what was there to complain about? She had a fireplace laid ready to light, enough vodka for a tangy gimlet, and the latest John Grisham novel to read. She'd be just fine.

But Courtney couldn't help noticing the warm patch of light and soft music that filtered through the pines from Amy's cottage, and she couldn't help wondering whether the arrogant little blond was snuggled in front of Lincoln Spencer's fire...or in his arms.

****

"Auntie Court!" The small, pale boy flung himself toward her almost before Lisbet's red Volkswagen came to a complete stop in Courtney's pine-lined gravel drive.

"Andrew John Grant!" Lisbet squealed, killing the motor. "For heaven's sake, you'll get yourself killed!" She tumbled out and rushed to Courtney, encircling her with plump arms. "Hello, Lovely! You're even prettier than ever. Door County must be good for you!"

Courtney held Lisbet off at arms' length for a second before pulling her close for a warm hug. "Little Sister. It's so wonderful to have you here! How have you been?"

"Making it okay." Lisbet smiled, but Courtney noticed the smile didn't reach her eyes. And it looked as though Lisbet had been overeating again as she always did when things got rough. Not really fat, but she definitely had added at least fifteen, maybe twenty, extra pounds.

"It hasn't been easy," Lisbet said. "But," she tilted her softly-frizzed brown head at Andy, who was gripping Courtney in a breath-stopping hug around the waist. "We'll talk later, after you-know-who is in bed."

"You-know-who's not sleepy!" declared Andy. "I want to go water skiing."

"Water skiing! You can't!" Lisbet declared. "He's too small, isn't he, Courtney? I told him you'd say he was too small."

"Oh, you did, did you?" Courtney laughed. "Don't you put me on the spot, Liss." She looked down at Andy. "We'll talk about that later, too, okay, Champo?"

Andy made a face and then grinned as he hopped around her and pulled on her hand. "Later, later. Let's go. Where's the water? I want to see your boats!"

With Andy running ahead, Courtney and Lisbet walked the half-block down the path to the weathered store building thirty feet from the softly lapping water.

"Do you have boats?" asked Lisbet. "I don't know what you do or don't have. All I know is that Courtney's Sports is going to open next week and set this place on its ear."

Courtney laughed, hugging Lisbet around the waist as they walked. "Don't I wish. Oh, Liss, I'm so glad you've come. Half the fun of work or play is sharing and I've been alone practically ever since I got here."

"Haven't you made any friends? Or have you just been too busy. I know your landlady died. Did that affect your buying the property?"

Courtney made a face. "I'm not without a landlord, it seems." They made the last turn in the path and were nearly at the corner of the store when

Courtney stopped walking. "And *lord* is the operative word. He's Amy's nephew, a big-shot lawyer from Chicago, who inherited all her worldly goods. And part of that is a half interest in Courtney's Sports until I pay off the down payment." Courtney frowned. "I offered to buy him out, but he said no. What I'd have used, I don't know, but I certainly don't need, or want, him giving advice. I hope he leaves soon. Surely he won't stick around a little place like Sister Bay for long. Anyway," Courtney continued walking, "he's handsome as sin and overbearing as—as—"

"A teddy bear?" Lincoln Spencer stepped around the corner of the store. He smiled, his teeth white against his already tanning face. "Hello! I couldn't help overhearing. I liked the *handsome* part," he grinned, a most attractive man at his pleasant best, "but I thought it better to make my presence known before you finished the second."

Courtney let out an exasperated sigh. Why did he always turn up at the most awkward moments? At the same time, she noticed that his trim-fitting sports shirt and matching blue shorts accentuated his well-built physique, and in spite of herself, couldn't help agreeing with her own *handsome as sin* assessment.

"See what I mean? Lisbet, this is Mr. Lincoln Spencer. My sister, Lisbet Grant. And that young blond whirlwind that probably passed you on his way to the pier is her son Andy."

Lincoln inclined his dark head and smiled at Lisbet, as though meeting her was an honor he hadn't expected. "Welcome to Door County, Lisbet. Will you be staying long?"

"Most of the summer, I hope. That is, if Courtney will put up with us. We've rented our own cottage up the way." Without taking her eyes off his face, Lisbet waved a plumpish arm in the direction

18

of Sister Bay's Main Street.

Watching the interchange, Courtney nearly gritted her teeth. All his kind had to do was smile and women fell at their feet. Lisbet's unfaithful husband already hurt her enough. She didn't need anybody new using her to bolster his male ego.

"Was there something you wanted, Mr. Spencer?" Courtney asked, pointedly stepping around him to continue toward the store.

"It's Link, please. Just a little company, is all."

"I would have thought you had more than enough," Courtney blurted in spite of herself.

He looked puzzled, then threw back his head and chuckled. "Oho, you must have met Miss Georgie Burns. Ah, yes." He grinned at Lisbet, tilting his dark head toward Courtney. "Miss Iceberg here won't be friends. Suppose you could put in a good word for a lonely lawyer on sabbatical?"

"Sabbatical!" Courtney's eyes widened.

"That sounds like more than a vacation," said Lisbet. "How long are you staying?"

Please, not long, thought Courtney, clenching her jaw. Go back where you belong.

"Only a few days right now, but I'll be back." Lincoln Spencer put his hands in his shorts pockets. "I deserve some time off, and things could be pretty interesting around here. And—" he rolled his eyes sideways at Courtney, "don't I have to keep an eye on my half of the business?"

Courtney brushed past him. "Please excuse us. I do have work to do, you know." At the door she inserted her key, furiously rattling the knob to open the stubborn old lock. Lincoln Spencer annoyed her so much she could hardly stand it, and yet—she glanced back at his dark head bent over Lisbet's lighter one—he was the first man she'd met since Ronnie's death that made her breath come faster.

She wasn't ready for that. She slammed open

the door. I won't be. And he's not going to hurt Lisbet, either. I'll see to that.

Chapter Four

"Well, you certainly weren't very polite." Lisbet looked back over her shoulder as Lincoln Spencer strolled toward the water. She followed Courtney into the store. "Couldn't you be friends? Is he an ogre in a handsome prince disguise? A frog in drag? Come on, Court. Does he deserve that kind of treatment? If he does, I want to know why."

"Oh, Liss." Courtney made a face. "I guess he really doesn't. It's just that every time I've seen him so far he's put me in such an awkward position." She didn't elaborate on the incident on the beach. "And he's so damn sure of himself." Courtney broke off, waving her arm to include the whole display floor. "Well, here we are, Courtney's Sports. What do you think?"

Lisbet's eyes, duplicates of Courtney's but darker blue, widened as she turned to get the benefit of the showroom merchandise from fishing tackle to water ski equipment. "Wow! I'm impressed! It's beautiful. But how did you know what to stock?" She fingered a display of colorful boat cushions. "All this fishing stuff? We never fished when we were kids."

Courtney grinned. "You're absolutely right. I didn't know a thing, but I read a lot—wait until you see the assortment of books I've got up at the cottage—and Amy was a great help. We ordered most of this before she died. Her husband had been in the business, and she'd helped him run it." Courtney's eyes clouded. "I wish you could have met her, Liss. She was just the kind of person we'd have

21

wished our mother to be."

"Really? Then I'm sorry, too. I can't even imagine having a real mother—except you. I was so young when ours died and you were always right there for me." Lisbet sighed. "I've learned since having Andy how tough it must have been for you, raising me when you were hardly more than a kid yourself. Don't think I'm not aware of the sacrifices you made to make my life better." She frowned. "Sometimes..." she broke off, shrugging.

"Sometimes, what?"

"Oh, I guess I just wish I knew more. About mothering. It's sure no snap. I never know whether I'm doing the right thing for Andy. I guess...no, I know, I hover over him too much, but—" She hurried to the store's large, many-paned front window, breathing a sigh of relief when she spotted Andy on the dock with Lincoln Spencer. "He's all I've got. If anything happened to him..."

"It won't. Don't look for negatives, Liss. We're going to have a good time this summer, and Andy will, too." Courtney put her arm around Lisbet's shoulder and they watched through the window as Andy and Lincoln Spencer walked to the end of the dock, Andy pulling on Spencer's arm and pointing down into the clear water.

Courtney snorted. "Listen to me. It's easy to give advice from an aunt's point of view. Now, what I don't know is what to do about my landlord there. Bet you anything he'll try to tell me how to run my store. And it is mine even if it's not all paid for yet." She paused, frowning. "What I don't understand is, if he always wanted to have the fishing business, like he says, why didn't he? Why am I so lucky to be saddled now with somebody who has preconceived ideas about what should or shouldn't happen here?" She studied the tall, assured figure on the dock. "I'll tell you, Liss, I'm glad he's going back to Chicago, even if it's only for a while. I don't know what to think about him. Or even how to act around him, I guess."

"You don't know what to think! Well, I can tell you what I think. I think he's about the best example of a man I've seen in a long time!" Lisbet raised her eyebrows and grinned. "And I can tell by the way he looks at you that he could be interested. Why not be nice? You could do a lot worse than that hunk of masculine poetry."

"Thanks," Courtney said dryly. "But you can have him."

Lisbet turned her rounded face to Courtney's. A series of speculating expressions chased each other across her features. Then she pursed her lips, put both her hands on her ample hips and grinned again. "Well, it's a little soon to tell, but I just might take you up on that, sister Courtney. I just might give Mr. Lincoln Spencer a go."

The screen door burst open and Andy charged into the store, his light blond hair askew. "Auntie Court!" He threw himself at her, nearly knocking her off her feet.

"Whoa, Champo! What's the hurry?"

"Mr. Link—" Andy turned to his mother, "—that's what he says I can call him, Mom, so don't say I can't. Mr. Link says there's fish right under that dock, and that right now is the time to catch them!"

"Oh, he does, does he?" Lisbet smiled.

"Yes! And he says Auntie Court's got all the stuff in here to do it!" Andy hopped from one foot to the other, his blue eyes widening as he looked around the room. "I sure do guess he's right. Can I? Can I, okay?"

"You might get hurt, Andy, get yourself hooked. You don't know how," Lisbet protested, putting a restraining hand on his frail arm. "I think you should wait."

"Oh, Mom." Andy sighed, turning to Courtney. "Please, Auntie Court? All I need, Link—Mr. Link—says—"

Courtney looked toward the man on her dock. His legs were widespread, like they had been when he stood over her on the beach. One arm shaded his eyes as he watched a small sailboat bob across the bay. With different clothes, in a different setting, he could have passed for a Viking explorer searching the horizon for land.

"Aren't you listening, Auntie Court? A pole and some string, and a hook, and some bait. He says you've got worms, too. Have you?" Andy pulled Courtney's hand. "Please, don't listen to my mom, she can't fish."

Courtney laughed and gave his thin shoulders a hug. "Well, let's see if you can. Here." She pulled a short cane pole down from a display. "This one is all fixed up for somebody just your size. The worms are in that box outside the door, and Mr. Lincoln Spencer can just go ahead and bait your hook for you, since it's his idea. Okay?"

"Okay! He will! I know he'll show me how to do it myself, too. He said he would! Thanks, Auntie Court!" Andy dashed out the door, scrabbled for a couple of worms from the box on the wide porch and covered the thirty feet between the store and the shore in seconds.

"Oh, one more thing!" Courtney called from the door to the running figure as he reached the dock. "Your Mr. Link can clean them for you, too, if you catch any. If he knows how."

Andy stopped short, looking up at Lincoln Spencer. "Do you know how?"

"I believe we can manage," he said shortly, turning to walk toward the end of the dock.

In the store, Lisbet studied Courtney curiously. "How to make friends and influence landlords?"

"Sorry." Courtney shrugged. "He's just so damn self-assured. Come on. Let's go up and think about supper. I'll bet you're hungry after your drive. We'll have a drink, and I've got some fresh perch and homemade potato salad for later, okay?"

"Great." Lisbet followed her out the door, shading her eyes from the afternoon sun. She called to the pair on the dock, "We're going up to the cottage, Mr. Spencer—Link. If you're not busy, will you keep an eye on Andy until he's done fishing?"

"Will you, Mr. Link? Okay?" Andy asked, his small voice anxious. "Else she'll make me go with her now and I want to fish!"

Grinning, Lincoln Spencer looked down at the frail boy. "Sure, Mom," he called back, smiling as he tousled Andy's hair. "Don't worry about a thing. Us guys are going to catch a few of these fish before the sun goes down."

****

Later, Lisbet and Andy's things had been moved into their log cabin a block up the graveled road and Andy had been protestingly put to bed after helping Link clean the two small sunfish they'd hooked.

Courtney and Lisbet curled up on the maple-armed chintz-covered couch in Lisbet's main room and toasted each other with a glass of cherry wine.

"Cherry?" Lisbet had asked. "That's different."

"What else, for your introduction to Wisconsin's Cherryland?" Courtney smiled, lifting her glass to touch the rim of Lisbet's. "To your future!"

"And yours!" Lisbet answered, smiling back. "Here we are, on our own again. Seems a long time since we've both been in this position, doesn't it?" She stared into her glass, swirling the clear ruby liquid to catch reflections from the small fire Courtney had set to take away the early evening chill. The silence grew heavy with their separate thoughts until Lisbet said, "What do you think our futures hold?"

Courtney listened to the night sounds of Door County, the wind sighing through tall white pines, the soft lapping of bay water down at the shore, and insects creaking a slow, early summer song. She stared at the flickering fire. "Who knows? Whatever it is, I'm going out to meet it." She put up her chin. "Ready or not."

Lisbet nodded. "That sounds just like you, always knowing what you want and how to go about getting it." She bit her lip and shifted her weight to tuck her legs under her. "I wish I could be so confident. I was so sure I wanted Richard—and so sure he wanted me. Nobody—not even you, Courtney—could tell me anything. And when they tried, I just went ahead and got pregnant so he'd have to marry me. What a mistake that was!"

Courtney leaned forward to touch Lisbet's arm. "But Andy's no mistake, Liss. He's a real positive. Your statement on belief in the future, I guess." She got up, rolled a log over in the fireplace and watched as sparks darted up the chimney. "I've often wished Ronnie and I had children."

"I always wondered why you didn't. You were married for more than three years."

"Ronnie didn't want them." Courtney shrugged and put the poker back on its stand. "All he wanted was fun and excitement, not being tied to anything except me. I was a kind of trophy, I think now. Something he could wear on his arm. 'Look, see my pretty wife watch me race!' or something like that. He was more my child than my husband in some ways, but God, how I miss him!" Courtney reached for the white-jacketed bottle of Von Stiehl and filled both their glasses to the brim again. "Well, enough of that. Ronnie's gone, and I'm here and I'm moving on. At least I think so." She smiled. "I'll know more about that after this first summer in the store, won't

I? It has to be a success, if for no other reason than to get my lordly landlord paid off! And what about you?"

"Good question. Richard will support me, he says, until Andy's eighteen, or I remarry." Lisbet frowned. "Will I ever find another love? I'm taking Richard at his word, though I can't imagine why. Most of the words he told me over the years weren't true. After that, who knows?"

Courtney leaned forward. "For heaven's sake, Liss, Andy won't be eighteen for eleven years! Are you going to stay tied to Richard's purse strings for that long? Aren't you planning anything for yourself? School, or a job?"

"Oh, I don't know!" Lisbet nearly wailed. "This past couple of years has really thrown me for a loop. Everything I thought I wanted for myself, even for the three of us—a nice house, two cars in the garage—it all seems so superficial now. Was it?" She shook her head. "Even though Richard and I were separated on and off for three years, I just didn't make any headway in planning. It was mostly anger against his infidelities, and survival. I had Andy to take care of, and I didn't want to put him in day care. Maybe this year when he'll be in school full time...oh, I just don't know!"

"You sound like a high school senior trying to decide whether there's really life after the prom. Haven't we had this conversation before? More than once?"

Lisbet made a sucking noise. "You're right. I am going to stop feeling sorry for myself right now! This minute! Back to basics, where do we go from here, not where have we been and how was it. Right?" She waved her glass at Courtney, who laughed.

"Right. First things first. And that means, for me, some sleep. Bright and early tomorrow I have to get my three boat motors—this is not a big operation—in running order. I want to be ready for the customers that will come for Blossom Time and the Memorial Day celebration. That's the real beginning of tourist season here, I'm told. If the weather cooperates."

"That's only a couple of days away! Oh, Court, I meant to tell you but it slipped my mind until right now. Maybe you won't be thrilled—" Lisbet broke off, frowning.

"What?" Courtney raised her eyebrows.

"Well, I ran into Jerry the other day."

"Jerry! Jerry Mitchell?"

"The very one. He wants to see you. He's coming up to stay through the weekend."

"Here? With you?"

"No, Silly. Somewhere up the road, nearer the center of town. In a condo, I think he said. He just wants to see you, check up on how you are, he said. But there's more to it than that, I think. You know Jerry's always been crazy about you."

Courtney made a face. "That's all I need, another macho man around telling me what I ought to do. He'll probably do just that, you know, under the guise of what's best for me."

"You can handle that. Tell him—oh, hell, Court, let him squire you around a little. That wouldn't be so bad, would it? He's just an old friend who cares how you are."

An old friend, thought Courtney, staring into the fire that changed with lightning swiftness in her mind to the real horror of that last day at the Indiana track. She shut her eyes against the pain of remembering Ronnie's race car careening into another, two-wheeling across the track, slamming into the barrier and bursting into flames.

Jerry, standing beside her at the fence, had turned her face to his muscled shoulder so she wouldn't see the medics pull Ronnie's flaming body from the wreck. Jerry had stayed through the nightmare hours at the hospital and helped make arrangements for the funeral. He had done everything he could to get her through those horrible days.

"I can handle things, Jerry, really I can," she'd said. "You don't have to do everything for me. Take a break. Get away."

"You've got to let me help. He was my life, too. You know that."

Yes, she had. From the time he and Ronnie came together as amateur racers they had been a close as—maybe closer than—brothers. And Jerry always had the money to subsidize the racing cars, pay the entry fees for Ronnie as well as himself. She didn't blame him for Ronnie's death, that wouldn't be fair. But Jerry Mitchell was, would always be, a reminder.

"Court?" Lisbet's voice brought her back. "Hello? Earth to Courtney!" She reached out to touch Courtney's arm. "Are you in there?"

Courtney shook her head. "Sorry. Back in time, I guess. A time I'd just as soon not go back to." She got up, walked to the window and stared out at the star-sparkled black night over the bay. "Tell Jerry not to come. Not now, anyway. Not yet."

Lisbet put down her glass and made a face. "I'm sorry, Court, but it's too late. He's already here."

Chapter Five

Later, back in her own cottage, Courtney lay wide awake. The soft night sounds that usually soothed her to sleep seemed too loud, the sighing pines too mournful, too lonely. Sheer window curtains moved quietly as moonlight sifted through the whispering trees.

She turned her face to the wall, picturing Jerry, his flyaway hair, his slightly misshapen nose from a racing crash. His sturdy body, hardly an inch taller than her own always seemed a little out of place in sleek racing clothes. His stature never hampered his ability to please the crowd, though; the sidelines were always filled with shrieking young girls when Jerry raced. Of course he reveled in their admiration, though he never did more than kid around with them.

"They're cute, sure," he'd commented to Courtney after one winning race when he'd been squealingly besieged for autographs. "But they're babies. I'd like 'em more than half my age, y'know?"

Courtney moved restlessly and plumped up her pillow. Why did he have to show up now, a living, breathing reminder of all the things she was trying so hard to forget?

But she knew the answer. Jerry had always wanted to be more than a friend. There were hints of that even while Ronnie was alive, though Jerry had cared too much for Ronnie to pursue those feelings. But there was always a little extra touch when she handed him a drink, an especially warm hello or good-bye hug, and the knowledge that his eyes always followed her from across the room.

Jerry had never been less than a perfect gentleman, as well as the solid leaning post she'd so badly needed during the terrible hospital days, and through and after Ronnie's funeral. Jerry had even been there to share her sorrow when she scattered the pathetically small box of ashes to the winds on the hill high above Ronnie's favorite track.

It was only months later, on her last night in Milwaukee, that Jerry left no doubt as to his hopes. He'd taken her to Karl Ratzsch's elegant and famous German restaurant. She'd declined, at first. "Thanks, but no, Jerry. It's too soon. I don't want to go out, especially not to any place as fancy as Ratzsch's. McDonalds, okay."

Jerry ignored her refusal. "Don't be silly. Who knows when I'll see you again? You deserve a send-off, a fitting start for your new life, and you're going to get it. I won't take no for an answer."

And so they'd gone. As he predicted, their quiet, candlelit table with a string quartet's soft music filling in the silences had been just right for a send-off. They talked of Ronnie, of past good times together. Of the future.

"You'll come down for the Indy Five Hundred again, won't you, Courtney? All the old crowd will be there. They'd all love to see you, especially me. You aren't going to be glued to Door County, are you?"

There was no hesitation in her answer. "No, to answer your first question, I won't come down to that race. Or any other. Never again. And yes, I'll be glued to Door County. Please understand, Jerry." Courtney leaned toward the candlelight. "I never want to stand at the sidelines again, watching people drive themselves into oblivion." She'd shivered and rubbed her upper arms to warm them. "I don't ever again want to feel guilty for being glad when the driver in a crash isn't someone I love. Besides," she smiled to take the edge off her words, "that race falls at the beginning of my tourist season, and in case you don't know, the golden rule for us storekeepers is, be here when those tourists are!"

"But I...damn it, Courtney! You can't just drop out of my life like this. It was bad enough losing Ronnie. Not you, too. You know I hoped—" Jerry had stopped himself, took a drink of his deep red Burgundy, and, after a moment, grinned and resumed his usual offhand manner, "Anyway, after all we've been through together, how can you get along without me?"

She laid her hand on his. "Jerry. Thank you for caring about me, and about our friendship. But you'll always be part of the racing scene, it's in your blood. And I want no part of that."

Jerry had looked at her over his glass, his blue eyes as serious as his words. "Without Ronnie and you? I don't know." He shook his head, unsmiling now. "I could give it up, Courtney. If I had a reason."

She threw back her head and laughed. "Like you could give up breathing, no doubt. Whatever would you do?"

He scowled. "Go ahead, laugh. Believe it or not, I have a teaching degree. History. You didn't know that, did you? You thought I was just a racing playboy. I could teach. Tell those little buggers about the Alamo, or World War II, whatever. Or I could do nothing at all, if I chose."

"Ah, the advantages of the independently wealthy!" Courtney teased. "To work or not to work, no matter." Her thoughts flew to her own precarious financial situation. What would she do if Courtney's Sports flopped? Every cent she had was wrapped up in it. She'd sighed, and touched Jerry's hand again, lightly. "But you don't have a reason to stop racing, Jerry. Don't be foolish. Live the life you love. I intend to." There was more bravado in her voice than she really felt. Making the jump to Sister Bay was what she wanted...wasn't it?

Their final goodbye that night was warmed by mellow German wine and shared nostalgia. At her door, Jerry held her tightly for a long moment. She'd hoped he wouldn't kiss her, and he didn't.

Instead he pushed her to arms' length and stared at her in the light from the porch lamp as if he would memorize every inch of her face. Then he said, "I know you feel you've got to go away now. I understand that. But I'll be waiting for you. As long as you want."

Courtney had stepped back from the emotion in his voice as well as the implication. "Don't say things like that. W-we're buddies!"

"Sure." He nodded and grinned his lopsided grin, taking the tension out of the moment as he stepped down the short flight of stairs to the sidewalk. "That we are." He had paused at the bottom and looked up before saying quietly, "Is that enough? For you?"

Enough.

Courtney turned restlessly, attempting to pound her pillow into a more comfortable cushion, while Jerry's parting question echoed in her mind. Was friends enough? From Jerry, yes. But she wanted more, surely, sometime. She was young; her body was warm and capable of taking—and giving—love.

She gave up on her pillow, knowing sleep wasn't about to come with so many memories tumbling over each other in her mind. Finally, she slid out of bed and pulled a short robe over her nude body. A moonlight swim in the cold bay water would clear the cobwebs from her brain.

Slipping her feet into beach thongs, she eased the screen door closed and walked the narrow, shaded path to the shore. The moon was so bright that although the sky was unclouded, the stars were scarcely visible.

Courtney kicked off her thongs and let her robe whisper to a tumbled heap on the pebbles. She reached up to secure her hair on top of her head as she stepped into the cool, quiet water; a slim, silvery nymph wading slowly into moonlit ripples.

****

A short distance up the shore, in a paneled two-room fishing cabin thick with a smoky haze combined with the smell of good brandy, five men in their late 60's hunched over a scarred, round oak table. The centerpiece was a pile of red and blue chips, the blue each representing one hundred dollars, the reds fifty. One empty brandy bottle lay on the floor; a second one, half-filled stood on the table.

A large, wheezing man chewing on the stub of an expensive cigar riffled his cards and threw another red chip on the pile. "Raise you, Ted." He coughed, a phlegmy gurgle behind his hand.

"Hmmmm." Ted Vogl studied his cards for a few seconds and inhaled from a long, dark cigarette. "You're on, Adam." He carefully placed another red on the pot.

"Fold." The dark, foreign-looking man at Vogl's left threw his cards face down. "God, Adam, do something about that cough. Sounds like you're dying!"

"Fold here, too," said Hank McKee. "We're *all* dying, Jem. That's one of the reasons we're working together. So we can die in comfort." McKee's grin showed a gold incisor. He ran a stubby hand back over his bald head and scrubbed his ear with his palm as he looked toward his left. "Lucius?"

"I'll stay." Lucius Bray tossed a red chip onto the pile. "Show."

Judge Adam Burns fanned his cards on the tabletop. "Three queens. Any better? Ted? Lucius?"

"Hell." Ted Vogl snorted, biting his mustache with his lower teeth before slapping his cards down. "Adam's been takin' it to us all night. You'd think he was planning to retire on his winnings. Let's get to the meat of this meeting." He smiled lopsidedly at his own play on words. "Lucius? Got him beat?"

Bray shook his head. "Two pair. Kings and fours." He sighed. "It's all yours, Adam." He pushed his chair back. "And you've held us off long enough. What's the word?"

Even the act of raking in his chips was an exertion for the large man. He tongued his cigar to the side of his mouth, paused to fill his lungs, then lifted his glass as his gaze moved around the table.

The four men leaned forward as one.

"Gentlemen," said retired judge Adam Burns, "I've found our man."

Chapter Six

"Here you are!"

Startled, Courtney looked up from arranging various fillet knives in a glass-topped display and recognized wild, tow-colored hair above a familiar smiling face.

"Jerry!" She straightened her striped tank top, brushed her palms on the legs of her jeans, and held out both hands. "Lisbet said you were coming. No, that's not quite right. She said you were here." Courtney studied his face for any trace of emotion left over from their previous parting in Milwaukee. "If you'd have asked, I'd have said stay away. But it's good to see you."

"Well, I didn't ask, you didn't say it, and I'm here. God, you're looking wonderful. Let me feast these old city-tired eyes. Sister Bay must agree with you." Jerry pulled her toward him and gave her a healthy smack on the lips that changed to a warm, lingering kiss before she pulled away. "I've been waiting for that for months," he said. "It was almost as good as I hoped."

"Same old blarney." In spite of herself, Courtney smiled.

"Let's try that again," he said, with his familiar tilted grin. "Only this time try to be a little more enthusiastic, could you?"

Courtney laughed. "You'll never change, will you? Forget it. This is a business establishment, you know."

"Glad you realize that," Lincoln Spencer said

stepping into the showroom from the door toward the water. "Mixing business with pleasure is never a good idea."

Jerry stepped away from Courtney, whose breath had caught at the sight of Lincoln's confident figure. She stopped short of stamping her foot. The man always appeared without notice at the damndest times!

"Lincoln Spencer," he said easily, putting out a hand to shake Jerry's. "Courtney's business partner."

"Really?" Jerry appraised Link's well-turned-out sports clothes. After a moment's hesitation, Jerry took the extended hand and added in a cool voice, "I didn't know she had one." He turned to Courtney. "What gives? Have I come in during the second act, or what?"

Courtney sighed, pushed a flyaway strand of hair from her forehead with the back of her wrist and shook her head. "Jerry Mitchell, meet Lincoln Spencer, my self-appointed business partner. Believe me, he wasn't my idea. I'll explain him to you later."

"Over a drink and dinner? It's just about that time," Jerry said. "I'll pick you up in an hour. There must be some nice eating place here in this tourist heaven."

Before Courtney could open her mouth, Lincoln stated, "She can't go."

"Can't!" Courtney echoed, frowning, her arms akimbo. "Really, Mister Spencer. Have you also appointed yourself my social secretary?"

He smiled, his teeth white against his darkening skin that was in such contrast with Jerry's city pallor. "I came to remind you that you've got a date with me at a fish boil. Remember?"

Courtney slid her hands into the back pockets of her jeans. "Date! Hardly a date! Oh, Jerry, I did promise to go to the boil. But you could come too, I'm sure. Couldn't he?" she asked Lincoln, who shook his head.

"Afraid not. It's for the Sister Bay business people only. Tough luck, Mitchell."

"For one of us," Jerry muttered.

"It *is* for the business people. I'd forgotten. And as this is my first season as shopkeeper, I guess Courtney's Sports needs to become part of the local scene." She turned, her chin up, to Spencer. "Since as you can see I have company, and since you're so anxious to declare yourself my partner, you can go for both of us."

"That wouldn't do. You're going to want the other shops to recommend your place, and you're going to need to make friends and influence the natives if Courtney's Sports is to be a success." Lincoln continued, "Aside from their curiosity about you personally, they're going to want to hear about your shop. No, we'd better be there. Together, as planned. The cocktail hour starts at six. I'll drive. Sorry, Mitchell."

Jerry watched Link's tall, confident figure stride out the door. "Sorry, he says. Overbearing bugger, isn't he?" Jerry frowned. "Lincoln Spencer. For some reason, that name sounds damn familiar." He paused, then turned seriously to Courtney. "Say, you aren't—I mean, is he—? Oh, hell, are you—? I mean..." He stopped fumbling for words at the incredulous look on her face before she burst into laughter.

"You mean am I interested in Mr. Big—the G.C.L.—that stands for Great Chicago Lawyer?" Courtney stepped to the door to make sure Lincoln was really out of earshot. "Anything *but* interested. Let me tell you how and why Lincoln Spencer came into my life."

****

Three hours later, as the western sky darkened,

Courtney stood with Lincoln and a group of Sister Bay business people in a cheerful firelit circle surrounding a large, smoke-encrusted fishboil kettle. Surprised at the size of the crowd, she studied her fellow shopkeepers. Courtney hadn't realized how many there would be, representing everything from small galleries to large and expensive gift shops, from stores selling hardware supplies to drugs and souvenirs. Dress varied from the usual blue jeans and open-necked plaid shirts on the younger artisans to classic sports clothes like those Lincoln Spencer wore so easily. Courtney's printed cotton skirt and loosely gathered white blouse fit in casually between the two extremes.

The boil was held on the waterfront village park close to the center of Sister Bay where picnic tables had been set up to take advantage of the view of the water. In one hand Courtney held her second gimlet; in the other she balanced a plate of tiny, spicy meatballs.

Courtney was unaware of the approving glances that appraised the couple they made: he tall, dark, intense; she slender and blond. Her attention was held by the big, red-faced, pot-bellied cook whose white chef's hat and apron gleamed in the fire's reflection. He blew a shrill blast on a silver whistle hanging from a cord around his neck.

"Stand away! Boil time!" he shouted, and flung a measure of kerosene onto the snapping, crackling wood under the pot. The crowd stepped back as one, expressing a collective "Ooooohhhhh!" as the flames roared and flared into an eight-foot burst, boiling the liquid in the kettle over its top in a bubbling mass; then breathing "Ahhh!" as the fire below sizzled to smoking remains. The spectators broke into approving claps and laughter and streamed toward the groaning buffet table. In a matter of minutes traditional steaming platters of freshly-boiled lake trout and the potatoes cooked with it were spread out among dishes of coleslaw, baked beans, colorful gelatin molds and other sumptuous dishes prepared for the hungry crowd.

"Ummm. I love fish boils," Courtney said as she heaped her plate. "Aside from tasting grand, the boilover itself is an entertainment, like fireworks. We always used to find a boil to come to when we vacationed here." Courtney sobered, remembering Ronnie, as she and Lincoln settled with laden plates at one of the long trestle tables arranged to overlook the bay.

"Fireworks? Oh, you mean the oohs and aahs. Well, we aim to please here in the County," said Spencer. "It's a special place, as you must know, having decided to hang your hat and future here." He poured coffee for them both from a Thermos pot on the table. "You're not sorry for missing your dinner with Mitchell?"

Courtney made a face, then smiled. "Not really. I'll see him later. Anyway, he'll be here for a couple of days. Besides, this *was* important to introduce the store. Wasn't it?"

"I thought so. And important for other reasons, too. But you'll have to judge that for yourself." Lincoln turned to respond to a greeting from someone behind him and Courtney was left to answer her own question.

Around them others settled in, many stopping for a "Great to see you back, Link—going to be able to stay a while?" or offering condolences on Amy's death.

"Your Aunt Amy must have been well known and loved," said Courtney, helping herself to more baked beans.

"She and Uncle Tom were mainstays of this little community," said Link. "It's not that big, you know, under a thousand year-round people. But I don't need to sell you, do I?"

Courtney glanced around at the tables of laughing, congenial people. "No, you don't. I felt like this was home the first time I came here, and the feeling grows deeper every day."

"You vacationed here with your parents?"

"No. My husband." Courtney hesitated. Then, feeling a need she didn't understand, confided, "H-he was killed. Racing." Courtney stared out at the water, her voice low. "I always hated it. The chances, the hurts..." She straightened her shoulders. "Sorry. That's over. And I'll never be part of the NASCAR world again. Never!"

Lincoln's grey eyes held hers compassionately for a moment before he deftly turned the conversation to include an older couple, gallery owners from the area bordering the town, with an invitation to join their table. Conversation moved to predictions for the season and soon the couple regaled their dinner companions with hilarious tales of early art-bargain hunters, until an older man put his hand on Link's shoulder.

"Heard you were back, Lincoln. Good. Goin' to put down some roots now, are you?" He gave Courtney a piercing once-over and nodded approvingly. "Hope so. Need some feisty young blood to help in runnin' this show up here." He tipped his cap to Courtney and was lost in the crowd before Link could answer.

"Roots?" Courtney questioned.

"That's Jeff Castle," Lincoln laughed. "Pay him no mind. He's been trying to talk me into Door County politics for years. He's an old friend of my Uncle Tom's." Link pushed his plate away. "We've made our appearance here. Want to take a walk down to the piers and work off some of these calories?"

Courtney sighed, smiling. "Great idea. Good

heavens, I think I ate enough for a week."

"You aren't alone. A person could get fat in no time, lazing around here."

She hoped he wasn't planning on that.

They walked to the end of a dock. Small ripples slapped softly against the wood and fiberglass sides of the early season sailboats and launches moored there. "Later this summer there won't be an open berth at any of these piers," Lincoln said.

"Good. Maybe lots of them will need fishing gear," commented Courtney, enjoying the quiet away from the enthusiastic crowd. A light breeze played with her clothes, fluttering them against her body and loosening tendrils from the braided coronet around her head.

She looked from the harbor scene to Link's face. "Beautiful here, isn't it? There's something about water that always rejuvenates my soul, no matter how down I get. Look!" She pointed at a brightening speck over the western horizon and, closing her eyes, chanted softly, "Star light, star bright—"

She sensed him move closer and her breath quickened.

"Better hurry," he teased, "before another star appears or your wish won't come true. What is it you want, Miss Courtney? Riches and furs?"

Her clear laugh rang across the water. "Lord, no! Is that how you see me? If I believed in stars, I'd wish for a summer's worth of lots of fishermen and good weather."

"What a romantic you are," Link said dryly, thrusting both hands deep in his pockets as Courtney, deliberately not looking at him asked, "And how about you, Mr. Spencer? You seem to have your world well in hand. What do you wish for?"

He was quiet for a moment, studying her profile, before turning abruptly toward the shore. "Wishes are for dreamers. It's getting chilly. Shall we go?"

Chapter Seven

The next morning Courtney and Lisbet drove through back roads separating the many sun-sparkled cherry orchards that dotted the county. Small, unobtrusive signs pointed the way to art galleries, jewelry and pottery workshops. A slight breeze moved the clear, invigorating air laden with the sweet, light scent of thousands of cherry blossoms.

"I've never seen anything like this!" breathed Lisbet, leaning forward for a better look at orchards clouded with white-frosted trees. "It's beyond imagination!"

"Isn't it?" Courtney agreed as she deftly drove toward Rowley's Bay and Newport State Park on the northeastern side of the peninsula. "And, as they say, you ain't seen nothin' yet. The cherry trees are only a part of it. Door County's a lot like a little New England. Roll down your window and smell this fantastic air. I knew you'd enjoy seeing some of the local terrain, and us natives—get that, I'm claiming Door County citizenship—are right proud of our cherry trees. Especially now when every one of them is bursting with bloom."

"I guess!" Lisbet leaned back in the wind from the open window and breathed deep of the perfume-laden air. "I'm glad we left Andy with Link. Just a few hours of being me instead of Mom is heaven." She gave a worried glance at Courtney. "He'll be all right, won't he? You do think so, don't you? Link is being so generous with his time."

Courtney competently braked around a sharp

turn and headed north. "Of course Andy will be fine. He had big plans for fishing this afternoon. Your Mr. Link remembered where he *always* used to catch great perch, and they're going to take one of the boats out to see if the descendants of those long gone are still there to be caught." She smiled. "Don't you worry about Andy. He's having a ball. And I think Link Spencer is, too. I think he's trying to do for Andy what his Uncle Tom did for him when he was a kid."

"I didn't know they were going on the water!" Lisbet frowned, then laughed at herself. "Probably a good thing I didn't. He will wear a life jacket—won't he?"

Courtney patted her sister's denimed knee. "Absolutely, Liss. It's a state law, and I certainly wouldn't let anybody in one of my boats without survival gear. Now, forget about Andy, and let's enjoy what's probably going to be one of my last free days until the tourist season is over. At least I hope I'll be so busy I can't leave."

"I hope so, too." Lisbet said. "Or else, as Link says, you're going to have a whole lot of inventory left when the tourists are gone in the fall."

Courtney felt a twinge at Link's name, and groaned. "*As Link says.* Don't remind me. Link *says* a lot, and much of it has to do with my store. I have to keep biting my tongue. Did Jerry find you last night?"

"Yes. He took me and Andy to a marvelous place in Fish Creek—what was it?—The White Gull Inn. Gorgeous! The food was great, the wine was wonderful...and all he wanted to talk about was you."

"That must have been boring." Courtney grinned and turned into the parking area at Newport State Park. "Grab that picnic basket from the back and come along. I want to show you the shoreline here.

It's magnificent."

Lisbet stopped with her hand on the car door. "Listen to me, Courtney. You know Jerry's in love with you. What are you going to do about it?"

Courtney pulled her hair into a barrette at the nape of her neck. She grimaced and tugged on a tennis hat and slammed the car door. "Absolutely nothing. He's a good friend and I care for him a lot. But he'll just have to get over it. I've got no room in my life for a man right now and I told him so, especially not one that's in any way connected with the racing crowd. Clear?"

"Clear to me. But he's really a swell guy. And moneyed. You could do worse. He's really hoping, you know." Lisbet's rounded face broke into a grin. "There! He asked me to put in a good word, and I did. Now, let's see your shoreline!"

Laughing, sisters in spirit as well as blood, each holding one handle of the laden picnic basket, they scrambled over the pine-needle-covered path to where Lake Michigan waves thundered against and under the rocky twenty-foot bluff.

Mesmerized by nature's unrelenting force, Courtney and Lisbet stood together in the spray at the edge of the rocks. Caught up in the power of the spectacle, they watched the waves crash, fall back, crash again. The wind was chilly, but not cold. Courtney put her arm around Lisbet's waist and hugged her. "Thanks for coming, Little Sister. Your being here is going to make my summer."

"Mine, too," said Lisbet. "And with any luck—" she made a thumbs up sign with her free hand, "—a couple of other people's, too."

"Oh? Whose, for instance?"

"Andy's, for sure. He's already opening up. And his color is really improving." Lisbet tossed small pebbles into the foaming waves before continuing.

Courtney felt an unwelcome twinge in the pit of

her stomach and reached for the picnic basket. "I'm hungry, Liss. Let's get to that chicken."

****

Late the next day, Courtney smiled as she stood looking into the afternoon's waning light, remembering the earlier comfortable interchange between herself and Jerry Mitchell before he left to go back to Milwaukee. There's a lot to be said for comfort in a relationship, she thought, comparing her tumultuous pairing with Ronnie and the awkwardness she felt at even being in the vicinity of Lincoln Spencer.

"I'm here to steal you away for the day, Courtney," Jerry had said as he snapped the store's screen door closed behind him. "What are my chances?" Hands in his shorts pockets, he rocked back on his sneakers as he waited for her answer.

Smiling, looking up from a price sheet of reels and tackle, she shook her head. "Not good. I have a lot to do, and tomorrow is the big day."

"I thought you'd say that. So, here I am, ready and willing to help instead. Even dressed for it, see?" He pulled on the leg of his denim shorts. "How's that for a compromise?"

"Oh, Jerry, you nut. I thought you'd be gone by now. How long are you staying?"

"As long as you'll let me."

"Be serious."

He waggled a finger at her. "You don't like me when I'm serious."

She couldn't help laughing. "Really. I am serious. You must have something you have to get back to Milwaukee for."

"Nothing more important than being here, wooing you."

She closed the catalog. It was impossible to discourage Jerry. He was like a friendly puppy, always underfoot and wagging its tail. She laughed and handed him a screwdriver off the countertop. "I give in. Lend a hand with fixing that droopy awning over the front window, then."

"Your slave, Madam," he said, making a courtly bow.

Jerry had fixed the awning, tightened the railing on the short steps, stayed long enough to help her put the final bits and pieces of the store in order and then picked up a takeout meal from a downtown eat-shop and brought it back. Fueled with hearty corned beef sandwiches and a bottle of robust wine, they'd sat on the rough wooden steps of her cottage's tiny porch. Below lay the store and the ever-changing bay beyond.

"Ummm. Delicious!" she declared, washing the savory spices down with swallows of wine.

"Glad you like it," he said, lifting his glass. "What I really wanted was to take you someplace special tonight, sort of a before-the-grand-opening celebration. The Yacht Club over at Bailey's Harbor, or someplace special in Fish Creek. This..." he indicated his sandwich, "runs a poor second—or sixth."

"You know, it's kind of funny," Courtney said slowly, leaning her elbows on her knees as she stared into the distance over the water. "A couple of years ago, I don't think I'd have said this, but I don't really need the fancies any more. My life has changed. I'm off the fast track in more ways than one. Corned beef and Swiss cheese suit me just fine." She paused, as vignettes of restaurants, hotels, racecourses from the past that now seemed so distant filled her memories. She shook her head and brought her mind back to Jerry. "Liss said the Inn was super. She really enjoyed her evening with you. Thanks for giving her something special."

"My pleasure. Lisbet's a good sort. Cute and funny. Andy's a fine little kid, too." There was more behind his words, a sorrow Courtney couldn't quite define.

"You were married before I met you, weren't you?"

"Yes. For a very short time." He was quiet and Courtney didn't interrupt his thoughts. "Sally died. Having our son. He died, too." Jerry shook his head, leftover pain darkening his eyes. "Jason Jerry Mitchell. God, Courtney. He was so little. So helpless...he'd have been a little older than young Andy now."

"Oh, Jerry, I'm sorry! I didn't know."

He smiled then, and put his hand over hers. "Sally was a lot like you in some ways. Not in looks. She was little and dark. But she felt the same way you do about racing." His eyes clouded and he stared out over the quiet water. "Funny, isn't it? She always thought I'd get killed. And she's the one who's gone." He sighed, straightened his shoulders and smiled his usual *everything's okay* smile. "But that was a long time ago, centuries, it seems, sometimes. And here we are, and now what?"

"You're going home to your pet fish and I'm staying here hoping somebody will want to catch some whoppers with my equipment. That's what."

"That's not what I meant, and you know it."

She felt the emotion underlying his voice, though his warm, tilted smile made light of it.

"Don't say it. Don't get serious on me. I can't handle it."

"You don't want to."

She met his eyes directly. "It's been great to see you, and wonderful to have your help and to have a meal where fishhooks aren't staring me in the eye. Can't we leave it like that?"

"Guess we'll have to. For now, my little chickadee." He sketched a leering WC Fields gesture that made Courtney laugh, and tossed a piece of crust to a friendly ground squirrel. "By the way," he continued, pouring the last drops of wine into her glass, "I've remembered why Spencer's name sounded so familiar. It's from a couple of years ago. I think you'll find it interesting that your friendly partner is the lawyer that so brilliantly defended the race driver that ran Buzz Jones into the rails at the Daytona track. Remember?"

Courtney thought for a moment, then shook her head. "No. Not really. But from what his Aunt Amy said, he could probably have successfully defended John Wilkes Booth. A veritable paragon." She wrinkled her nose. "Let's talk about something else. What will you do when you get back to town?"

"Same old stuff. Get greasy. Check out a new model—car, that is—I've been told about. Do some time trials on a so-called super vehicle for a group of anonymous investors."

"Why anonymous?"

"Who knows?" Jerry had shrugged. "Rich people are often eccentric. You can bet, though, if I win they'll spread their names as well as the amounts in their bank accounts over all the headlines from California to Maine."

He'd hugged her then but hadn't tried to kiss her. "I'll be back whenever I can make it. I've got a lot of tests to run on this new car. Wish me luck?" His blue eyes probed deep into hers with so much open longing that she had to look away.

"Oh, yes. All the luck in the world."

It had been a relief to see him go. Too many memories. And too much emphasis on a future she would never be part of. Never.

Courtney's thoughts were interrupted by a small whirlwind that hurled itself around the corner, through the door and grabbed her around the waist. "What're you doing right now, Auntie Court, and can you guess where I'm hiding?"

"Oh, you've thought of a good one, have you? Let's see, let me guess. I get three questions first, though, remember, before I have to try." Courtney smiled affectionately at Andy, pleased that he enjoyed the *let's pretend we're hiding* game that she and Lisbet had invented. They played by the hour when Lisbet was young and quarantined first with chicken pox, then mumps. Altogether they had spent the better part of two months confined to the house.

"Is it dark where you're hiding?"

"Sort of. Sometimes." His eyes twinkled with the secret.

"That's not much help. Is it wet?"

"Sort of. Part."

"Great." Courtney punched him lightly on his upper arm, noticing as she did that Lisbet was right, he was already developing considerably from rowing her small fishing boat up and down in front of the dock. He'd added some weight, too. Now if he could only conquer his tendency toward asthma when he was upset. "Well, I get one more question. Are you standing up?"

"No, it's too short." Andy giggled and hopped from one dirty tennis shoe to the other. "You won't guess, I know you won't guess."

"You're under the bench in the tool area of the storeroom."

"Nope! You get two more guesses."

Courtney closed her eyes and made a wild attempt. It was always more fun if she was wrong. Andy loved to outsmart her. "You're under the dock."

Andy's face fell. "Darn it, Auntie Court, you almost always guess. One time I'm going to find a place you'll never think of!" He sighed. "Okay, your turn. You hide. Oh!" He ran to the door. "Here comes my mom and Mr. Link! Hey!" He ran to the door. "Here I am in the store!"

Courtney and Andy pushed through the screen

door and Andy ran toward the approaching couple whose heads were together in an easy companionship. They were dressed in *town* clothes and it looked as if their lunch hour, which had evidently stretched a good deal, had been spent agreeably. Courtney had refused to accompany them with the excuse that she had to mind the store, but that was only part of it. Lisbet needed a clear field for pursuit. And, Courtney admitted only to herself, Lincoln was too unsettling. She didn't feel at all comfortable with him, yet she couldn't have put into words exactly why.

Courtney studied the pair as they walked toward her. From all appearances, it seemed that Lisbet's plan to change Lincoln Spencer's life was well under way. She looked up at him and said something, with a soft expression that was new to Courtney. Love? Well, Lisbet will have a formidable competitor in Miss Georgie Burns, who had stopped in earlier looking for Link and hadn't been pleased to hear that he was having lunch with Lisbet.

Andy grabbed Link's hand and pulled him toward Courtney. "Now can I learn to water ski, can I? Are we going to let me now?"

"You know I said no!" said Lisbet. "You're not strong enough. And besides, it's still too cold."

"Right," confirmed Courtney. "Another couple of weeks, okay, Champo? Then we'll talk about it. That will give you more time, too, to beef up those arm muscles from rowing. Water skiing really takes a lot of strength."

"Aw." Andy's expressive young face clouded with disappointment.

"When I get back, Andy," said Spencer, ruffling the boy's fair hair. "We'll give it a go. I promise."

Courtney felt a wretch somewhere inside. "Oh! Are you leaving?"

His smoky eyes studied her face for a moment.

"Do I detect a note of hope in your voice, Partner?"

She flushed, not meeting his eyes. "Of course not. I just wasn't aware. How long will you be gone?"

"He'll be back for the Fourth of July celebration. And then he can stay for a while. Won't that be grand?" Courtney watched as Lisbet looked up at Lincoln Spencer's tanned profile with open adoration, and noted with annoyance that he seemed perfectly comfortable basking in its glow. Evidently Lisbet's plan was going better than expected.

If that's what Lisbet wants, Courtney told herself, I hope she succeeds. But Courtney didn't ask herself why, if that was really how she felt, she found it so hard to be glad for her little sister.

Chapter Eight

Late that same afternoon, Courtney glanced out the store's wide front window. The earlier breeze had died and the water was smooth with a grayish cast. Not good fishing weather, she thought, and wondered whether she should pull up the unrented fishing skiff. It didn't look as though anyone would be taking it out now, and having it already on shore would give her one less thing to do at closing time.

She put aside the sporting goods catalog she'd been studying and was just about to open the door when Georgie Burns rounded the corner, wearing the world's tightest, shortest white denims and a brief white bra top. With her was a large man, tall and heavy, bordering on obese. His rotund body was encased in red shorts and matching cotton shirt that made him resemble an oversized cardinal. His legs, toothpicks in comparison to the width of this body, did nothing to relieve the image. An enormous black cigar sprouted from one corner of his mouth and he carried an expensive-looking fishing pole in the other. An obviously well-worn, tied-fly encrusted hat was pulled down to keep the lowering sun from his eyes. In spite of his top-heavy weight, he walked with authority. Georgie's companion looked like a man who always had things go his way, or else.

She stepped toward the door to ask what she could do for them when Lincoln Spencer's voice preceded him down the path leading up to the cottages. "Judge Burns." Lincoln's voice was colored with respect as he held out a hand to shake the older man's. The quiet late afternoon air carried their voices clearly into the store through the open door.

"Been waiting to see you, Lincoln." The judge's voice, a raspy growl that ended in a bronchial wheeze, sounded as though he had smoked too much for too long. "Are we on for a fishing hour or so?"

"Certainly, if you wish," Lincoln answered easily. "Unless you'd rather talk in my cabin." He indicated the cottage at the top of the hill.

Judge Burns looked up to where Amy's weather-beaten cabin nestled comfortably among the pines. "I think not. Ears."

"Ears?"

"I'd prefer we weren't overheard."

"Oh, Daddy!" Georgie pouted prettily, twisting a sandaled toe in the sand. "Can't you talk later? I wanted Linky to take me for a boat ride!"

Linky! Boat ride! Courtney snorted to herself. If Lincoln Spencer thought he could just take a boat any time he wanted and keep away her paying customers—she looked around but didn't see any—he would just have another think coming.

She started out the door to set things straight when Georgie said, "Let's take that big boat, Linky, nobody's using it, and whiz around the bay. You could show me all the sights you remember from growing up here." She wrinkled her nose up at him. "God knows that wouldn't take long, but it's something to do. Anyway, it's your boat, isn't it? You don't have to ask permission from—" she tilted her head toward Courtney's Sports and Courtney involuntarily stepped backwards inside the door, "that store—clerk person, do you?"

Courtney made a face. Store-clerk person!

"Now, Baby," the Judge rumbled, clearing his phlegmy throat. "You can talk to Lincoln later and maybe then he can take you for a ride. Right now he and I have some business to discuss."

Georgie pursed her ruby red lips and tilted her head, then slipped her arm familiarly through Lincoln's, pretending to be unaware that her bare thigh rubbed seductively against his sharp-pressed flannel slacks.

It's like watching a soap opera, thought Courtney, not even considering that she was openly eavesdropping. After all, the three of them were standing out in plain sight right in front of God and Courtney's Sports. She stared, fascinated. The vamp in action, marking her territory even though there was no one there to challenge.

"I'll see you later, then, Georgie," said Lincoln, moving unobtrusively but definitely away from the pressure of Georgie's sun-warmed leg.

Her father nodded, wheezing. "That's right. Be a good little girl, Georgie, and go back to the hotel. Aren't they having some kind of a doing during cocktail hour? A fashion show or something, it said on the board today." The judge mouthed his dead cigar and winked conspiratorially over the girl's head at the younger man.

Georgie's pout turned into a smile like sun coming out after rain. "Really? Fashions? Oh, fun!" She put her hand on her father's thick arm. "Daddy, give me your American Express card!"

Judge Burns chuckled, an odd gurgle that ended in a wheeze and cough, as he tossed his cigar stub into the water—bringing a scowl to Courtney's face—and fished the card from his thick wallet. "Now, Baby," he said, patting her solidly encased denim behind, "You just go and have a good time. I'll be back after Lincoln and I finish our little talk, and you can show me what you bought. How about getting a pretty new dress for when we take you out for dinner tonight? Something that will really impress our Lincoln, here?" He chuckled again, smiling benevolently at her obvious pleasure.

Our Lincoln?

Like a child on the way to an ice cream sundae, Georgie stood on tiptoes to kiss her father's florid cheek. Then, putting both petite little hands behind Lincoln's neck, she pulled his dark head down to her blond one, whispered something into his ear and gave him a lingering, moist, open-mouthed kiss.

Inside the store, Courtney frowned, then laughed aloud. How could any intelligent man be taken in by such a demonstration of the ultimate coquette?

Pretty easily, she answered herself, watching Lincoln's gaze follow Georgie, as she nearly skipped to a long, black Lincoln Town Car parked at the end of the store. After beeping the horn two resounding toots, and daintily fluttering her red-tipped fingers at the men, she deftly turned the machine around and headed back toward town, the hotel and carte blanche with Daddy's American Express.

Courtney guiltily realized her eavesdropping when she heard the judge say, "Now, Lincoln, the fishing. Where we can't be overheard." She opened the screen noisily and walked to where they stood near the dock, nodding to Lincoln and putting out her hand to the older man. "I see you have your own equipment. May I help you with a rental?"

The judge studied her for a moment before pulling a second cigar from his mouth with one hand and accepting her firm handshake with the other. His puffy eyes traveled the length of her trim figure in denim shorts and plaid shirt, down her slim legs to her well-worn canvas boat shoes. "This the partner?"

Courtney mentally gritted her teeth, waiting for a smart response. But he only made the introductions. "Courtney James, Judge Burns. Is the skiff reserved, Courtney?"

"No."

"Then we'll take it."

"Certainly." She looked pointedly at his fine dress slacks and open-necked sport shirt and his lack of a fishing pole. "Going fishing in those?"

"Do you always check out your customer's apparel?" he asked, amused. "What a discriminating clientele you must attract."

"I only meant—" She broke off, cheeks flaming, hoping she hadn't revealed overhearing their earlier conversation. "Certainly the boat is for hire. Seven-fifty the first hour, five for each succeeding."

"I thought this was your business, too, Lincoln," the Judge questioned, his heavy-lidded eyes openly appraising the interchange.

"No freebies from this partner. She's a tough business person to the death. My worldly affairs couldn't be in better hands. Clock us, Courtney, we'll pay on return."

"No freebies, huh," she muttered aloud as she watched them push the boat away from shore. He'd better believe not. Freebies could fritter profits away, and she had no intention of shorting the business. Not while she still had part of a down payment to return to Mr. Lincoln Spencer, she didn't.

Courtney smiled. Things had been going well these first few days, and if they kept doing so in the future, she wouldn't be indebted to him for very long at all.

And that would please her greatly.

****

The water was grey and slickly quiet as the small skiff chugged its way out, riding dangerously low in the water with the men's combined weights. Lincoln cut the motor and it sputtered to a stop well away from shore. He waited, listening to the small sound of water lapping against the boat's wooden sides. The judge had called this meeting, and he would speak when he was ready.

Judge Burns made no pretense of putting out his fishing line. Instead, he reached for a gold monogrammed lighter and, after going through the pre-smoke ritual of biting off the end, licking the dry outer leaves and smelling the pungent aroma, lit up a new cigar. "Now, Lincoln," the judge finally wheezed, leaning forward with both hands braced on the edge of the boat. "What's your answer?"

Lincoln hesitated briefly. "To which question?"

"Both of them. The corporation, first. Wincar."

Link looked out over the slate-grey bay toward the dock at Courtney's Sports, where Andy sat cross-legged on the pier, dangling his short line in the water. "To the question of the business arrangements, yes. It will be a challenge to draw up the legalities for you and your group."

"It's bigger than that. We've talked it over. We're offering you full participation."

Lincoln looked up quickly. "How? I can't afford it."

"You can't afford not to have it." The judge took a long drag from his cigar, coughing, exhaling and spitting a piece of tobacco onto the water before he spoke. "Let me lay it out for you, Lincoln. We want you in on the investment but you haven't got the ready cash." He held up a beefy hand to stop Lincoln from speaking. "Don't interrupt. I've looked into your finances and I know what I'm talking about. You have a fine practice but it doesn't leave you eighty thousand to throw into the corporation. Okay." He leaned forward, his breathing loud in the quiet air. "So for your on-going legal advice at no salary, you'll be a full participator. Meaning that when we split the winnings pot with its accumulated earnings at the time I turn seventy-five, five years from now, you'll get your share to do with as you please." He slowly lowered a thick index finger to mash a mosquito feeding on his arm, then flicked its body into the water.

Lincoln shook his head. "Why me? You could get any legal beagle for less."

"I've got my reasons. And because I've watched you." Judge Burns' eyes narrowed. "You can handle anything we ask. Your reputation's clean. And we know you'll give us exactly what we want."

"And that is?"

"Nothing more than a legal corporation whose investments will assure five old men enough money to continue to live comfortably." He studied Link. "And that will give you, and your family, which I hope you'll soon have, enough to live on in the manner you'd like. It will also give you enough capital to get into the political ring you've been yearning for. If all goes well."

"Is there some reason why it shouldn't?"

The judge stared into Link's grey eyes, his expression noncommittal. "You tell us. You're the corporation lawyer." He took a deep breath and gurgled a cough, spitting a glob of phlegm into the water. "Do you accept?"

Lincoln watched a gull swoop down and snatch a small minnow from the water's glassy surface, leaving a widening ring of ripples. "Give me some time. If my answer is yes, it's on one condition: that I remain personally anonymous to the racing world. Totally."

The judge sighed. "I don't understand why that's important to you, but I know determination when I hear it. You realize it may be difficult, maybe impossible, to keep quiet when we win. Which we will. We can't miss with this car, I tell you, Lincoln, it's the best. But we'll go along with you. For now."

You don't have to know why it's important, thought Lincoln, staring across the water to where Courtney was now gracefully beaching the other fishing skiff. 'She won't have anything to do with anybody connected with racing any more,' Lisbet had said. 'She was hurt too much.'

The judge was still talking. "We'll put together the other funds. The plans have been approved and the car's construction is almost in the final stage. We want this buggy ready for next year's Indy, maybe sooner." The Judge gurgled and spit over the side again, wheezing as he sat upright. "One thing I insist, and that is I want the best driver available, somebody who'll give everything he's got for the big win."

"But not someone who'll risk the other drivers' safety," Lincoln stated quickly. He'd seen enough of racing disasters in his years as a railbird to last his lifetime. "No bad pennies."

"Fair enough. Do you have anyone in mind? You've done enough racing law and been involved behind the scenes enough to know who's good. And who can be had for what price."

Lincoln hesitated only a moment. "Matter of fact, I do. I met him just the other day, up here, in fact. If the car turns out to be as good as you think, he'll accept. It's Jerry Mitchell."

The judge spit a piece of cigar over the edge and was startled by a small bluegill that darted to the surface and sucked it in. "Look at that little bastard. Bet he's surprised at that tasty morsel," he chuckled. "Mitchell, Mitchell. Oh, yes, wasn't he a racing buddy of that driver that burned a season or so back?"

"Right." Lincoln looked toward shore, where Courtney had joined Andy on the dock. Even from this distance her slim figure and the independent way she moved was disturbing. How odd the connections of life, that he should be directly involved with Ronnie James' widow. That crazy, exciting fool had always taken too many chances, and the very thing that made him such a crowd pleaser had been what cost him his life.

The judge followed Lincoln's gaze to where Courtney now sat with Andy on the dock. His eyes narrowed. "Lincoln?"

"What? Sorry. Woolgathering." Lincoln brought his mind back to his companion. "Mitchell's good. Probably better than good. He's careful, but not one to hang back, especially if there's a healthy bonus laid on the winner. Not that he needs it—I've heard he's got money—but it's a measure of his ability as a driver. Ego stuff."

"Settled, then. We'll contact him."

Both men were silent for an awkward moment before the judge cleared his throat and opened the final subject that lay between them. "What about the other question?"

"That's a little more difficult, Sir." Lincoln brought his gaze back from Courtney's figure to meet the other man's eyes. "You know I've always admired you. First as a lawyer, then as a judge. I consider you one of the most fair men who ever sat on the bench. But you're not being fair now."

"All's fair in love and war, they say." The judge removed a bit of tobacco from his tongue and rolled it between his thumb and forefinger as he spoke. His usually authoritative voice didn't carry the same confidence in dealing with this subject as with the other.

Spencer didn't reply.

"You need more time for this, then, too. We'll discuss it later."

"I don't think that will change things, Judge." Link's gaze was drawn again to the figures on the dock. "In fact, I'm sure time will only deepen my feelings."

The older man's gaze followed Lincoln's for a moment before his expression grew hard. "I hope, for your sake, that you're wrong." The judge looked at his watch. "Start up that motor and let's get back, then."

As Lincoln reached for the starter cord, the older man held up his large hand. "But wait a minute." His puffy eyes narrowed and all joviality left his face. "There's one thing more you should know before you make up your mind. If you're really serious about moving up the political ladder, that is."

"You know I am. I've worked toward it for years." Lincoln waited, his hand on the motor.

"You're going to need my backing. And the active support of the four other men in Wincar. They're party people, and they carry a lot of weight. They do what I tell them. The men we support for office are the men who win. It's a jungle out there."

"I know that, Sir. I thought I had your backing."

The judge smiled slightly, the twist of his lips denying any warmth. "I don't think you're listening." He took a deep drag on the cigar, took it out of his mouth and pointed it at Lincoln. "Georgie means everything to me. Her mother's gone. You know I'm not well. I want to see her happy before I die. That's the uppermost goal in my life."

Lincoln frowned, pursing his lips. Then, as recognition of what the older man meant became obvious, his jaw hardened. "You'll withdraw your support unless I marry your daughter?"

"That's about it." The older man relaxed with a wheezy chuckle. "Just about it. I'm glad I didn't need to spell it out for you."

Lincoln Spencer started the motor with a white-knuckled grip on the starting cord before he said, "I think you've spelled it out quite clearly, Judge."

Chapter Nine

Early July morning sun was brilliant as Courtney, in brief crimson halter and rolled-up blue jeans, struggled in shallow water near her dock to attach a five horsepower motor to one of the two fishing boats.

"Damn!" Sucking on her pinched index finger as the boat skittered away into deeper water, she had to stop and roll her pants legs up another couple of folds. Why did the simplest tasks always seem to get out of hand? She'd done this dozens of times since opening the store. There was no reason to be awkward today.

Courtney didn't admit to herself that her clumsiness was probably due to lack of sleep. She had been ready to turn in last night when the lights flicked on in Lincoln Spencer's cottage. A shiver, then a warm flush had swept through her body, and, try as she might, sleep had been impossible. Too many thoughts swirled through her mind, now that he had returned. The two weeks he'd been back in Chicago had seemed long even though Courtney's Sports had kept her busy from dawn to dark every day.

Would he want to look at her receipts? Check her books? Generally stick his nose in where it wasn't wanted? How serious was he about this so-called partnership?

Most important, would he be kind to Lisbet? And to Andy, who had quickly turned to hero worship of his Mr. Link? Was he serious about spoiled, fluffy Georgie Burns? Maybe she was in his cottage with him right now. Maybe in his bed.

Disgusted that Lincoln Spencer was not only on her mind but occupying it fully, Courtney had switched on the light and read until dawn. If anyone had asked, she couldn't have told what the story was about, though she had methodically turned the pages.

Now she grabbed the back of the boat and bent to her work again, finally anchoring the motor in place. She clambered in, connected the gas line and, using an oar like a pushpole, shoved the boat a few feet from the pier where she could safely test the motor.

A pull on the starting cord did nothing. Another. And another. She set her jaw and reached for the cord again as a familiar husky voice asked, "Need some help?"

Startled, Courtney nearly lost her wavery balance over the motor. She sat down abruptly, steadying the rocking boat, and shaded her eyes against the sparkling morning sun. Lincoln stood on the dock, wearing tennis shoes, snug faded jeans and no shirt. There wasn't an ounce of fat on his muscled body and his bare, darkly-furred chest still held its earlier light mahogany tan.

"Maybe I can start it for you. I'm familiar with those things," he said.

Wasn't that exactly what he'd remarked about bra hooks? Courtney was annoyed at the flush that colored her face at the memory, and at the unexpected pleasure she felt in seeing Lincoln Spencer again. "Just what I need, advice," she muttered, almost, but not quite, under her breath. "Nice to have you back."

He grinned, undaunted. "Advice is my business, remember? I'm a lawyer."

"How could I forget?" She bit her lip and tried

the cord again, with no result.

"Choke it. It's not getting the gas."

Of course. She held in the choke lever, pulled the cord, and the motor sputtered into action. "Thanks," she said, gritting her teeth. "But I'd have worked it out myself in a minute. I've started these motors every morning since you left, you know."

"I'm sure. Just glad to help any time." His smile was broad, and guileless.

"I'll bet," Courtney said under her breath, bristling once more at his amused tone.

"How did your opening go?" he asked after she cut the motor and poled the boat back toward shore. He walked along the dock above her. "Were you swamped?"

"Not hardly swamped," she answered. She'd done just fine without his questions and comments for the past weeks. But he did own half of the store. So far. "Better than okay."

Actually, the grand opening of Courtney's Sports had been well attended. Possibly, she admitted, because of the coffee, cookies and small fishing lures she had given away, but she'd been pleased. And she'd had enough customers since to keep the store going. True, their purchases were sporadic, but that was all right; she was doing just fine.

She watched him walk the dock, sure-footed, and an idea surfaced. He was willing to help, was he? She'd find out whether he would put those elegant muscles behind his words. If he was so glad to be of assistance, he could lift the big motor onto the water skiing boat. It was always a struggle for her and Lisbet to get that one ready for use, and she had a reservation for it later in the morning.

Courtney deftly poled up to the dock, tied the rope with a quick half-hitch around one of the posts and looked up, giving him her most dazzling smile. "Are you for hire?"

Surprise lifted his dark brows. "If the price is right and the work is honest. What do you have in mind?"

She wrinkled her nose. "I might know you'd talk price first. Well, since you've declared your interest in the business, maybe you'd help me put the big motor on that boat," she pointed to a sleek, sixteen-foot white fiberglass model tied to the other side of the dock, "so I can check it out to my morning skiers."

"Will do, Ma'am," he answered, saluting smartly. "I just happen to be wearing my working clothes. "Where's the motor?"

"In the back storage room. There's a dolly there."

He strode off the dock, his long, lean legs covering the ground with assurance. Courtney's gaze followed him. No matter what else he was, she had to admit, as Lisbet had observed the first time she saw him, he really was a *fine example of a man*.

As if called by her thoughts, Lisbet, wearing a pair of baggy shorts and a faded green T-shirt that proclaimed "Milwaukee Summerfest," rounded the corner of the store. Her tightly-permed brown hair was still damp from the shower. "Morning!" she called, shading her eyes as she walked from the storefront toward the dock. "Beautiful day, isn't it? But going to be hot."

Andy, his thin but already leather-brown young body dressed only in blue boxer trunks, whizzed past his mother and leaped onto the dock. He leaned over the edge above Courtney in the skiff. "What're you doing in that boat, Auntie Court, and can I get in, too?"

"'Morning, Champo. Right now I'm getting out, that's what." Courtney pulled herself up onto the dock and made sure the boat's line was secure. "Maybe later you and I can take a spin." She laid her arm across his shoulders as they walked back toward shore.

"Why not now?" Andy put out his lower lip, then brightened and gave a happy little jump as he spotted Lincoln coming from the store with the large motor. "Mom! Mr. Link's back, see?" He jumped off the end of the dock and ran toward Spencer. "Mr. Link! Are you going to stay for a while now, like you said? Can we catch some more fish today? What're you doing? Are you working for my Auntie Court?"

"Sort of," Lincoln said. "Fixing this boat up for water skiing. Interested?" He pulled the motor from the dolly and hooked the clamps over the mounting board at the back of the larger boat.

Lisbet stepped forward but before she opened her mouth, Andy said, "I am. You know I already asked my mom. Lots of times." He paused looking sideways at Lisbet. "She didn't say yes yet though."

"Think she might?" Link winked at Andy as Lisbet stepped toward him.

"Just a darn minute there, Mr. Link." She put her arm protectively around Andy's thin shoulders and tried to look fierce while her face gave away her delight in seeing the man again. "You know perfectly well that his mom doesn't think he's big enough for waterskiing. Am I wrong? It's an on-going debate."

Courtney watched the exchange with interest, and a small pang of apprehension. The alive expression that lit up Lisbet's face on seeing Link was one Courtney hadn't seen since he'd been back in the city.

She wondered fleetingly what her beloved little sister was heading for. Another heartbreak? Lincoln Spencer was certainly a man who was capable of breaking. Or mending, she surprisingly thought.

Andy shrugged Lisbet's arm away, hung his head and pushed a bare toe into the sand. He looked hopefully up at Courtney. "Everybody keeps saying we'll talk about it later, Auntie Court. Is it ever going to be later?"

They all laughed at his disconsolate expression, and Courtney gave his thin shoulders a friendly squeeze. "Well, right now I have work to do, Andy, so I guess it isn't later yet. Besides, though the sun is warm that bay water is still pretty cold. And it takes two in the boat and someone on the shore to get you started."

"Can't Mr. Link come? And Mom can be on shore with me 'till the rope gets tight and I'm up on the water. I've been watching lots. I know how to do it, really I do."

"I'm available, Andy," said Link as he finished attaching the gas line to the large motor. "You convince these women, and we'll go at it. Later, when the boat gets back, and it's warmer." He raised his eyebrows at Courtney. "Right, ladies?" He looked encouragingly at Lisbet, whose cheeks flushed becomingly.

"No promises," she said, but Courtney would have bet she'd have given in to anything the man proposed. "We'll see."

"We'll see," Andy echoed. "We'll see. Lots of things we're supposed to see we never do."

"Link-y!" An accusatory high-pitched voice reached down the path from the cottages. "Oh, Linky, I was looking for you! You weren't at your cabin! I thought you'd never get back!"

"Whoo—ee! Who's that?" asked Lisbet, openly staring at Georgie Burns who was waving one bare bangled arm and carefully picking her way down the narrow path from the cottages to the beach.

She was wearing her floppy sun hat. The rest of her voluptuous figure was only constricted by a hip-hugging pair of shiny blue, very short shorts and a matching handkerchief-patterned bra top that only covered enough to keep her from being arrested. Her sandal's four-inch heels sank deep into the pebbled sand with every stop, making her approach anything but graceful.

Her voice continued as she neared the dock. "God, this place is like a tomb! Daddy goes fishing with his old buddies every day and plays chess every night with those old widows at the hotel. They're like living skeletons and every one of them is trying to be sooo sweet because they think he's got money or something. I mean it, they're like living, breathing skeletons!" She was nearly out of breath and stopped moving for a moment, but she didn't stop talking. "There's a ton of people around, but it's been so boring here without you, Linky!"

"What a body!" Lisbet whispered to Courtney, unconsciously smoothing her nondescript, faded T-shirt over her own ample hips.

Georgie continued to pick her way across the beach and warily stepped out of the unmanageable sand onto the dock, wrinkling her nose. "It smells awful down here. Like gas, or something."

Link, finished with the boat, secured it to the pier with a second line from the back and introduced Georgie to Lisbet and Andy, then said, "And I believe you're met my neighbor and business partner, Courtney James."

"Business partner! Oh, yes, the fishstore person. I certainly wouldn't have remembered her. I haven't been down here since you left." She gave a cursory nod to Courtney, who hoped her face wasn't smudged with motor oil. Georgie immediately went to stand in front of Spencer. "Do you really need a hobby up here, Linky?" she cooed. "Can't we just have fun? C'mon, let's skip out of here now."

Hobby! Courtney boiled inside. If that little lighthead knew the work that had gone into getting Courtney's Sports ready to open! And the hours to keep it going! She opened her mouth for an unladylike remark that was waylaid by Lincoln's smooth, "A flourishing business can hardly be called a hobby, Georgie. What's up?" As he spoke his eyes traveled lazily over her brief, skin-tight attire. "Has Sister Bay been good to you?"

Georgie did one of her pretty pouts and moved close enough to run one fire-red fingernail slowly and sensuously down the center of the dark hairs on his muscled chest. "Did you forget you promised to take me shopping as soon as you got back? And that we're meeting Daddy at Al Johnson's for lunch? I just love to see those silly goats on the roof." She looked up at him coquettishly from under heavily darkened lashes. Courtney looked away, but her gaze returned to the scene as though drawn by a magnet. It was almost laughable. Almost.

Lincoln caught Georgie's hand and pulled it away, saying easily, "No, my dear, I haven't forgotten. I said I'd pick you up at eleven, and I will." He moved easily away from her. "That is, providing you get dressed."

"Dressed! Everybody goes around in sports clothes here. Don't you like my outfit?" Georgie's mascared eyes rounded. "I thought you would, of all people."

"Cut out the games, Georgie. If you expect to be seen with me in public, put on something that leaves a little to the imagination." He turned the dolly around.

Georgie made a pretend face at his back, then turned and smiled sweetly at Andy. "Games are fun for any age, aren't they, Sweetie?" She minced her way to the shore end of the dock and stepped gingerly across the sand, trying to keep her spike heels from sinking all the way down with each step. At the bottom of the path she turned and waved her enormous hat. "I'll be ready, Linky! Eleven!" She disappeared up the hill.

"How come she called me Sweetie? And what'd

she mean about games, Auntie Court?" Andy squinted toward the path Georgie had taken.

Courtney gave him a hug. "Beats me, Champo. Step aside while we get this motor going. We don't want my business partner to miss his important shopping date."

"Your concern for my social obligations is touching." Lincoln gave her a long unreadable look before he continued to push the dolly toward the store.

****

"There's Daddy!" Georgie said, pulling at Lincoln's arm. "In the corner. Hi, Daddy!" The heavy silver charm bracelet on her slim bare arm jangled loudly over the restaurant's noontime clatter as she waved to the large man seated at a window table.

Lincoln squinted, acclimating his eyes from brilliant July sunshine to the dimmer interior of Al Johnson's crowded restaurant. He piled his armload of Georgie's purchases on the floor and extended his hand to the older man. "Hello, Judge."

"Lincoln. Good to see you back." The heavy man wheezed, pushing his coffee cup to one side of his placemat. "Sit down, Georgie, so I don't have to stand up."

"Sure, Daddy." Georgie pulled off her sun hat and slung it by its red flowered tie on the back of her chair. With a swirl of short matching skirt and embroidered petticoat, she sat, crossing her legs toward Lincoln and leaning forward so the scoop neck of her filmy blouse showed an expanse of bare cleavage to best advantage.

She looked like a life-size Barbie doll in her flowered sundress and high-heeled strapped sandals, thought Link. And she was like one in other ways, too. Pretty, but hollow.

"Oh, we've had such fun, haven't we, Linky? Daddy, wait 'till you see what I bought!"

"I can wait." The Judge smiled benevolently at her and winked at Lincoln. "Glad you had a good time. We'll have lunch, and then I want you to run along back to the hotel so I can talk to our Lincoln." He didn't watch Lincoln's physical wince at his use of the possessive.

Georgie put out a lower lip. "Talk, talk. Will you come to the beach later, Linky? You're going to love me in this new bikini. Wait 'till you see it, Daddy, there's nothing to it. It's just darling!" She turned the full power of her heavily mascared blue eyes on Lincoln and he immediately compared them to Courtney's unpainted ones that seemed to hold so much more depth.

"Linky? Did you hear me?" She turned to the Judge with an exasperated sigh. "Honestly, Daddy, he's like a walking zombie this morning!" She laughed nervously. "You'd think he had the whole weight of the world on him, like what's that statue? Adamus, or somebody."

"Atlas," Lincoln corrected her. "Sorry to be a less than perfect companion, Georgie, but there really is more to life than shopping for bikinis and baubles."

"They're not baubles," she protested. "They're things I need!"

Lincoln laughed dryly, and Judge Burns pulled his dead cigar from his mouth to chuckle with him. They both knew Georgie's necessities were things many women could easily do without.

"Sure they are, Honey, sure. Now, what would you like for lunch?" Judge Burns signaled a blond, Scandinavian-dressed waitress. "If you're hoping for a drink, Lincoln, they don't serve any hard liquor here."

"Coffee's fine."

They chatted about unimportant things, the number of sailboats in the harbor, the weather, the bustling tourists. Over their hearty sandwiches,

Lincoln described some particularly interesting artwork in one of the stores in the walking mall, and unusual pottery birdhouses in another.

"But it's nothing like shopping in I. Magnin's or Marshall Field's, Daddy. Two hours here and you've had it," complained Georgie. "Oh, I'll be so glad to get back to civilization!"

"I love it here," Lincoln said simply. "You would, too, Georgie, if you'd give it a chance. Try."

"I am trying, honestly I am. Maybe if you'd show me some more—" She laid her red-tipped fingers on his arm but he moved from her touch to pick up his coffee cup.

The gesture didn't go unnoticed by the Judge. "You don't have to stay here in Sister Bay just to keep me company, Georgie," the judge said. "You know that."

"I do have to stay here now," she said, looking at Lincoln from under long lashes. "Don't I, Linky?"

"Not on my account," he said, too quickly. Then, sensing the quick lift of the judge's head, smiled to soften his words. "I mean, of course if you're bored you'd want to be back in the city."

Judge Burn's narrowed eyes studied Lincoln's face. The boy was different, somehow. He'd noticed it the afternoon they'd taken the small boat out. Before this summer he'd seemed content to squire Georgie around to anything that came up. It had always been the judge's assumption that the merging of the two was only a formality. But now? Lincoln was obviously disenchanted, dragging his feet.

The judge looked from Lincoln to his daughter. Maybe it was too soon to have pushed that marriage idea...but how much time was left for a man whose lungs had turned against him? After Lincoln was well started on his political career and too caught in the Wincar corporation to get out would have been the right time. The other men hadn't wanted to give

Lincoln full participation, but Judge Burns had put in half the eighty himself. Dammit, he wanted Georgie to have plenty, and that was one way to see that she got it. If the marriage came about.

The judge pushed his plate away, wheezed as he moved his chair back from the table and pulled out a new cigar. Then he thought better of it and returned it to his pocket. "Run along, Georgie."

"Already?" She shrugged. "Oh, all right. Business, business. I'll be glad when you really retire and forget about anything but having fun!" She gathered up her armload of packages and with a swirl of skirt and a jangling blown kiss called, "See you later, Linky!" as she left the room.

The judge gargled a cough behind his hand. "Pretty little thing, isn't she?"

"She is that," Lincoln agreed. But that was all. The more he saw of Georgie Burns the less he appreciated. "What is it you wanted, Judge?"

"A report on what you accomplished in Chicago."

"Fair enough. I think you'll be pleased." Lincoln met the older man's gaze. "I've got the legal work for the corporation's articles arranged. Since I haven't yet met your cohorts, let me just briefly make sure I have the right men in the right spot."

The judge nodded and signaled for more coffee. "Fire away."

Lincoln ticked off on his fingers. "First, Red Vogl, Buyer at Rightgood Tires. Jem Feuerstein, Buyer for Miller Exhaust Systems. Lucius Bray, Purchasing Agent for Dunhill Sporting Equipment. Hank McGee, Warehouse Manager for Bocco Oil research. And you."

"And you. Same as the rest, one-sixth interest."

After hesitating just a moment as though he intended to protest, Lincoln continued, "The investment is eighty thousand per man. That amount will assure the car's construction and mechanic's salaries for first year."

The judge nodded. "What mechanic?"

"Tracer Bennet." Lincoln waited for the older man's reaction.

After a stunned moment, Judge Burns slapped the tabletop with the flat of his hand, then looked apologetically around the room. "Bennet! Christ, Lincoln! He's the best!" In his excitement the judge drew in his breath and choked. Heads near them turned in alarm, but as he coughed, red-faced, into his handkerchief, he waved one beefy arm to indicate that he was all right. "God, I hate that!" he said as soon as he could talk. "Sorry. How in hell did you get Bennet? Was it the salary? Or the car?"

Lincoln grinned. "Both, I think. He grabbed it so fast I almost got caught in the whirlwind."

"I thought the oil people had him sewed up for their new turbo-whatever that they've been bragging about."

"They thought so, too." Lincoln said. He looked the judge square in the eye. "As you well know, Judge, money does talk."

Burns sucked on his cigar and gave the younger man a long, meaning-laden look. "And don't you ever forget it."

Chapter Ten

Between renting out the fishing boats to three different parties, selling odd bits of tackle and bait and directing Andy's own private fishing endeavors while Lisbet napped, Courtney's afternoon was full. But it hadn't been too full for her to wonder whether Lincoln had taken Georgie Burns to Gage's elegant gift store for her shopping spree, whether they had wandered the little shops in the walking mall, and whether they had enjoyed their lunch at picturesque Al Johnson's. Probably Georgie had shopped there, too, in the Scandinavian Boutique. Courtney would have enjoyed a special lunch there herself on such a hot July day.

As she refilled the sinker section of the small fishing accessories shelf, she pictured the contented tri-colored goats grazing on the sodded roof of the restaurant and wondered if lingonberries were on this summer's menu as they had been other years when she and Ronnie had enjoyed them. "We'll come here every year after the Indy, since you love it so much," Ronnie had promised the last time they'd stayed in Sister Bay. "And you can eat your lingonberries until your teeth turn purple."

It was a special time. They'd laughed together and spent the quiet summer evenings walking the waterfront street from one end to the other, pretending that one of the two-masted sailboats moored beyond the docks was only waiting for them to come aboard and sail it into the sunset. They'd bought ice cream cones and sat on a bench near the piers until, content, they'd wandered back to their pleasant room at the hotel where they'd made love one last time before going back to the city. Courtney remembered their light-hearted joking about it.

But it really had been the last time. Less than a week later he was dead. And now she was here, alone. The unbidden wave of loss surged over her and she shook her head to clear the cloud of memories when she heard the wind chime announcing someone's arrival in the store.

"Busy?" Link asked from the door. He was casually but distinctively dressed in a pair of grey leisure slacks and a matching short-sleeved, open-necked knit shirt that made Courtney well aware of her own daily working jeans and blouse. Everything he wore seemed to accentuate the smoky grey of his eyes.

"More or less. Not right this minute. How was the shopping trip?"

"Successful, I guess, if the number of purchases is what counts. Though I doubt that I've convinced Georgie that Sister Bay isn't the end of the world. Personally, I can't think of any place I'd rather be. I hope some day to live here."

Courtney couldn't imagine Miss Georgie Burns living anywhere but the city. "Why does she stay if it's so boring?" she asked, though it was plain to her that Georgie's net was out for the man who stood across the room, and that she would do whatever it took to catch him. Courtney wasn't sure whether Lisbet—or anyone—could match that kind of fervent, moneyed competition.

"It's her father's old stomping ground. He used to have a cottage here, up the waterfront a way. When his health got too poor for him to take care of it, he sold it. But some of his old cronies still have property here, and he's rented rooms at the Hotel du Nord for the summer. His heart's still here."

"But hers isn't?" It was a two-edged question, but he ignored her obvious double meaning.

"Never was. In fact, she didn't even come here when her mother was alive. Now, she's here for her father."

I'll bet, thought Courtney, recalling the bright red fingernail moving slowly down Lincoln's chest, and wondering why he was here now. She hoped he wasn't going to start questioning her about the business.

"It's coming, Auntie Court!" A small voice shouted from the dock. "The big boat is coming back!"

"Uh-oh." Courtney stuck her hands in the back pockets of her white denims and went to the door, where she stood beside Link and watched the small boy hurrying to pick up his fishing things from the dock. "Guess what that means?"

"I don't have to guess. I know. It's finally *later*." He grinned down at her. "Come on, let's get the poor little kid on the skis before he bursts a blood vessel."

His open friendliness and Link's woodsy, masculine scent was distracting, but watching the excitement emanating from the small boy as he hopped up and down waiting for the boat to near the dock, Courtney smiled, too. "Why not? Andy's been a good little soul, not asking for much, and summer's practically half over. He deserves his chance. The weather's perfect. There's hardly a ripple on the water. It's a good time for him to start."

Link pushed open the door and, taking her hand, pulled her outside. Courtney had only a moment to experience the electric charge that went through her at his touch before it was gone as Andy, proudly swinging a stringer with two sunfish on it, barreled into both of them.

"Look what I caught, Mr. Link! Right under the dock! And I stringed 'em myself! Mom wouldn't touch 'em."

"Good job, Champo," said Courtney, admiring the little fish before she called to the swim-suited figure lazily sunning on a low chaise on the T-shaped end of the dock. "Liss!" The three of them walked out over the uneven boards toward her. "Wake up and let's get Andy on the water skis."

"I'm not sleeping," Lisbet answered from under the sun hat covering her face. As she pushed up the brim and sat up, it was apparent to Courtney that Lisbet's walking three miles a day had helped to take off the extra pounds she'd brought to Sister Bay. Her figure was definitely improving, and the new black designer suit she'd bought helped to disguise the few pounds that were left to lose. The healthy tan she was acquiring was a dandy. Courtney glanced sideways at the tall man beside her. Did he notice?

"Okay with you, Mom?" Link asked, leaning down to peer under Lisbet's hat brim and grinning as she squinted up at him. "He'll be fine. If he falls I'll get him into the boat so fast he won't even get wet."

Lisbet groaned and rolled over on her stomach. "I give up. I'm outnumbered. It's three against one." She smiled up at Andy. "And it's too hot to fight. Sure. Why not?"

"Wow! Really?" Andy plunked down beside Lisbet for a second, his blue eyes wide with surprise and anticipation, before he threw himself on her back and gave her a great hug. "Oh, Mom, thanks! I'll get my swimmersuit!" He was off the dock and up the path in a flash of bare feet and brown legs. "Don't change your mind!" he yelled from the top of the path. "I'll be right back!"

"He will, too, in a flash." Lisbet groaned. "You two had better get your suits on. I have a feeling you're going to have to pull him out of the water more than once. I'm serious. You know I couldn't save myself, let alone somebody else. I'll get him set on the skis and you two man the boat. And I'll take care of the store if anyone comes while you're on the water."

"They probably won't. It's a dull time of day," said Courtney. "But thanks."

It was only a matter of minutes after Courtney had checked the boat in and turned it over to her teenage helper for cleanup and refueling that Andy was back wearing his swim trunks, buckled into a small-size life jacket. He swaggered into the water with the shortest pair of rental water skis over his bony shoulder. "See, Mom? Mr. Link? This is how they carry these. I know."

"He should. He's watched enough people this summer," said Lisbet as Andy tried to keep his balance while fitting his feet into the unwieldy skis. "He's spent hours pretending he was gliding into shore after letting go of the rope. Looks funnier than anything, doing that on land."

"Look at Mom," Link teased. "She's right proud of the boy."

Lisbet flushed. "That doesn't mean I'm not worried. So there."

"Link-y!" The high voice called from the corner near the store. "Come here a little minute? Please?"

Courtney caught herself gritting her teeth. Georgie Burns, again. Just then a car door slammed shut behind the store and the back door chimes announced that someone had come into Courtney's Sports. "Excuse me," Courtney said, walking past the blond who now stood near the returned boat. "Business awaits."

Lisbet followed her into the store where Courtney talked to a burly outdoorsman about the difference of one fishing reel over another. As he examined the merchandise, she glanced out the side window and noticed that Link, after a very few words with Georgie, had started up the path toward his cottage to change into his suit. Georgie stood with her hands on her hips for a moment before she disappeared from Courtney's sight. Good riddance, thought Courtney. Let her go buy something with daddy's credit card.

The customer stayed for a good fifteen minutes before making up his mind. Courtney rang up the sale.

After he left, Lisbet whistled. "Whew. I'm impressed. When and how did you learn so much about fishing reels? I'm glad you were here when he came in. I'd have been no help at all."

Courtney grinned. "You'd have done just fine. Most of the time they know what they want anyway. They just want to talk about it first and let you know how smart they are."

"Aren't you all ready yet?" called an anxious voice from the water. "I am!"

"Poor Andy." Courtney hurried into her small utility rest room to shed her jeans and pull on the bikini that always hung on a hook by the door. "He's been waiting all summer for this."

A worried frown crossed Lisbet's face. "Do you really think he can do it?"

"Well, we'll find out." Courtney patted her sister's shoulder. "And if he can't, one thing's for sure, it won't be for lack of determination." Tying her long sun-bleached hair back with a ribbon, Courtney caught up a large beach towel. "Let's go!"

A few minutes later Courtney knelt, facing backwards, in the passenger seat of the large outboard as Link pulled ahead. "He's up!" she shouted. "And after only two tries! Great, Andy!" She made the victory sign with two fingers toward the little figure straining at the end of the rope as Link steadily brought the craft to a speed suitable for a young and inexperienced skier. Featherlight Andy seemed to fly over the top of the smooth water in the middle of the speedboat's wake.

"Oh, I'm so pleased for him! You should see the grin on his face!" Courtney, touching Link's arm to get his attention, yelled over the motor's whine.

"You should see the grin on yours," he answered, pleased at her excitement for Andy. "You do love that kid, don't you?"

Courtney nodded, holding back a wild rope of hair that had come loose in the wind. "Sure do. I always hoped to have a son. I wish Liss could see how proud he is. She'd love it, too!" Courtney grabbed her hair and held it over one shoulder to keep it from whipping in her face.

Link kept the boat at an even speed, glancing momentarily at the picture long-legged, slender Courtney made in her scanty suit as she knelt next to him, encouraging Andy to stay upright.

"Want to take a spin yourself when Andy's done?" Link shouted. "He could spot for you."

"Me? I haven't skied in years! I wonder if I even could!"

"It's like riding a bike. You never forget."

They made two relatively small circles in the bay before Link asked, "Think he's had enough? Are his legs shaking yet?"

Courtney waved to Andy and pointed toward shore, and laughed at his vigorous nod. "He's tired. Go on in."

They headed back, swinging wide so Andy could glide into the open area near the pier. "We'll see how well his landing practice does for him," said Link.

"Drop the rope, Andy!" Courtney called. "Now!"

Andy did as he was told and sailed to a smooth stop thirty feet from where Lisbet stood on shore before he lost his balance and fell backwards, spread-eagled, in a few feet of water. He came up grinning and floundered to the shore, sputtering, pulling the floating skis along behind him. Link and Courtney cut the motor and glided the boat in to the dock. Andy, wearing a grin the width of his face, dropped the skis on the sand and grabbed a smiling Lisbet around the waist, wetting her thoroughly before she wrapped him in a towel.

He hopped up and down in front of her. "I did it, didn't I, Mom? Did you watch me all around? See, I didn't even fall once! I told you I'm not too small."

"And you were right." Courtney climbed out of the boat to secure it to the dock, her smile as broad as the boy's. "Well done, Champo. Super job."

"I knew I could do it. And pretty soon I'm going to show you I can row that little boat all the way over to that place by that bluff, too, where those pretty rocks are. I can. Wasn't I great, Mr. Link?" Andy scrubbed the towel across his dripping face and beamed toward Link, who still sat at the wheel of the boat.

"Absolutely and positively just great. Better dry off before you get chilled."

"Okay." Andy ran up the path, stopping at the top to raise both arms, jump up and down and shout, "I did it!" before he disappeared behind the trees.

Courtney, Link and Lisbet grinned at each other before Link questioned, "Next?"

"It's getting too late," said Courtney. "Some other time, though. I'd forgotten what fun it could be to ride shotgun in a ski boat."

"Well, then, come for a ride anyway. Take a look at that sky." He waved toward the west. "It's going to be a spectacular sunset."

"Not me," said Lisbet, shaking her head decisively. "I don't even like boats. You two go ahead. I'll watch the store. I don't mind, really. Andy will be back in a minute. I'll close up at nine, as usual, and that won't be long. You don't have anything out that has to be checked in, do you, Court?"

"No. Not tonight." Courtney hesitated. Being on the water had been fun, speeding into the wind after such a long, hot day in the store. It wasn't likely that anyone would come this late, and, if they did, Lisbet could cope. She looked across the mirror-calm water to the western sky ribboned with streaks of mauve and orange. A jet stream climbed up out of the sunset, catching its colors and pulling them along in its wake.

The excitement of Andy's success made her a little reckless. "Well—okay. Sure you don't mind, Liss?" At the shake of her sister's head, she untied the rope and slipped down into the boat.

"We won't be gone long." Courtney waved to Lisbet and as Link maneuvered the boat away from the dock, she directed imperiously, "Take me to the sunset, James."

He answered, straight-faced, "Yes, Madam." Then, leering, he wiggled his eyebrows, stepped on the throttle and said, "And now, my pretty, you are in for a sunset you won't forget."

She shrank back in the passenger seat and squeaked, "Oh, Sir, are you the blackguard you portray? Help! Help!" She flapped her arms foolishly. "I'm being abducted to a sunset! Oh, help me, someone!"

He burst out laughing. "I quit. The frightened maid just isn't your style."

"I can't afford to have it be. Us businesswomen got to be tough!" But she laughed, too. The wind in her face felt wonderful, and the carefree feeling of being away from the responsibilities of the store had lifted her spirits almost beyond belief. "Where are you taking me to view this sunset that I can see perfectly well from right here?"

"Out to Little Sisters," he said. "I used to put up

my pup tent on those islands when I was a kid, and camp for the weekend with my buddies. There's nothing there but trees and rocks—at least that's how it was then—but we had wonderful times. The sunsets are magnificent from the west side. It's a couple of miles or so. Are you game?"

With a surprising recognition of the fact that she wanted very much to be right where she was, Courtney relaxed. "Why not?" Whatever their difficult circumstances, she was leaving them back on shore. The sky promised a spectacular show, the weather was balmy July, the man beside her was handsome and could be fun, if she let him.

Courtney sighed in weary contentment. Putting her hands behind her head and stretching her slim legs out in front, she smiled at her companion. She was going to enjoy this sunset.

And so was Lincoln Spencer. He headed the speeding boat into the bay, letting the wind blow everything from his mind except that he had Courtney James to himself and for once she seemed to have left her resentment of him behind.

He returned her smile. He would have to tread lightly on this relationship that had gotten off to such a poor start, but perhaps, just perhaps, this could be a beginning.

Chapter Eleven

As the sleek powerboat headed out onto the bay, the Western sky surged into an even more colorful display, adding streaks of magenta to its ever-changing violet and orange panorama. The lowering sun slipped behind a puffy purple cloud and rimmed it with a brilliant golden border. The water, quiet now, reflected every hue from the sky across its marble-smooth surface from the horizon to their speeding boat.

Courtney breathed deeply, tossing her head back and reveling in nature's beauty and the freedom that speeding across water always gave her—a total abandonment, as though any troubles or concerns she had were left behind.

The wind pulled the re-tied ribbon from her hair, letting her long tresses stream out behind her like those of a statue on the prow of an ancient ship. She put both palms on her temples to keep her hair from whipping across her eyes as she twisted in the seat to face Link. Her eyes sparkling with pleasure, she was a slim nymph-goddess in a scanty red bikini. She wore a mischievous, elfin expression he had never seen before, certainly not while she fulfilled her daily role of the professional businesswoman that ran Courtney's Sports so efficiently. She was always gorgeous, but right now, windblown and free of care, she looked beyond beautiful.

"Thanks, Mr. Link. I needed this," she declared, saluting him smartly.

His hands tightened on the wheel, but he only said lightly, "It's magic! You look like a different woman. What's happened to the shop-worn working girl I thought I knew? That *life is no monkey business* person that runs that store back there and hardly ever smiles at me?" He raised his heavy brows in question.

Courtney shrugged her tanned shoulders and grinned. "Gone. Out to lunch. Over the rainbow. Who cares?" She made a face at him. "And where's the tough, big-city lawyer who eats up the working girl and threatens to take away her store if she doesn't run it right?"

His jaw tightened. "There never was a person like that. He was the working girl's imaginary wolf at the door, that's all." He smiled disarmingly as he maneuvered the boat toward a small stand of trees rising out of the water ahead. "Friends?" he asked, quirking an eyebrow. "At last?"

"Sure. Friends." Courtney sighed with content, stretching her long legs before she jerked to a sitting position. "Hey! Hadn't you better slow down? We're practically on that island!"

"Oh. Right." He reluctantly pulled his gaze from her slim figure and swerved the boat to the left, rounding the western edge of the two islands and, cutting the motor, drifted easily until the hull touched bottom a few feet from a small sandy strip of land.

"All ashore what's going ashore," he said, stepping over the side into a foot of water and pulling the large outboard behind him to where he could tie it to a low tree with the bow rope. With a courtly gesture he offered his hand. "Coming?"

"You bet! The show's already started." Courtney bent to catch up the large beach towel she'd used to cover the sun-hot plastic seat. She reached out to put a hand on his shoulder to steady herself as she stepped over the rail but found her waist encircled as he lifted her easily from the boat. His strength was surprising and the warmth of his touch stayed with her even after he had put her down. Together they waded the last few feet of water.

After Link kicked away some sticks and tossed a couple of small rocks out of the way, Courtney spread the big towel at the water's edge in a narrow area beyond the growth of underbrush. A few chittering birds made evening settling-down noises in the undergrowth behind them. They sat cross-legged on the towel and quietly watched the spectacular sky as day majestically gave over to a balmy Wisconsin summer dusk.

Courtney leaned back on both palms and, though conversation seemed unnecessary, confided in a whisper, "I kind of expect to see God come down out of a sunset like that. It's too much, too beautiful." She broke off, giving her shoulders a little shake as she laughed at herself. "Silly, isn't it?"

As he watched her face, the long, slender neck holding her head so elegantly above her slim, tanned shoulders, he wondered if she had any idea at all of how lovely she was, and it took him a moment to bring his mind back to her question.

"No. Not silly at all," he said. "It reminds me of a painting Amy used to have. It was just a sunset, and I don't think it was religious, but it always seemed so to me."

They sat companionably as the sky lost its vivid colors, until finally, unfolding his lean legs, he stood up. "I suppose it's time we got back. Tell me, can you find your dock in the dark?"

Courtney laughed up at him. "You mean I'm out here in the middle of Green Bay with a navigator who doesn't know his way home?"

"That's about it." Link grinned and pulled her to her feet. "I'm just the pilot. You're the navigator."

She stopped shaking the sand from the beach towel. "But I thought you said you used to camp out here!"

"I did. But Uncle Tom always brought me out and came to pick me up. And usually in the daylight." At the alarmed widening of her eyes, he held up a hand and grinned. "Relax. I'm only kidding. I can find it, I'm sure."

"I'm only kidding, too," admitted Courtney. "I have a bright orange lamp on the end of the dock that's timed to turn on at dusk. I nearly lost one late fisherman before I put it in. So, Columbus, let's head for shore. It's way past dinnertime and I'm famished."

They waded back to the boat and, after Courtney was seated and the line untied, Link pushed the starter button and the motor sputtered into a cough before it quit. He pushed again, and this time the engine sputtered, caught, whined for a couple of seconds—and died. The third time it didn't even sputter.

"Try the choke," put in Courtney, enjoying his discomfort. "I know a little bit about those things." She wondered if he would remember his own words, and, from his obvious grimace, decided that he did.

"Cute. But this is going to take a little more than a choke lever," he said from the back of the boat. "It's going to take a full gas can."

"You're kidding!" Courtney's eyes opened wide and she flipped around, kneeling on the seat as she stared at him. "We certainly haven't used up a whole tank!"

"Wasn't it filled when that last couple brought it back before we took Andy out skiing?" he asked.

"It should have been. Bobby knew he was supposed to take care of that."

"Bobby?"

"My helper. That tall, thin teenager that's been

hanging around. Oh, you wouldn't know. He came into the store just after you went back to Chicago and asked if he could help. He trades with me. He wants to be able to use the boats to fish once in a while when they're not rented, so he's been running my errands and doing odd jobs afternoons. I suppose he could have forgotten." Courtney leaned back on her heels and frowned. "That isn't like him, though. He's been really conscientious."

"Evidently not conscientious enough," Link muttered.

Courtney caught her breath. "Oh, my. Lisbet will be sure we've drowned. She'll call out the Coast Guard and everything else."

"No, she won't. Remember? She said she was going to close the store at nine and head for a bath and bed." Arms akimbo, Spencer stared out over the water. "Our problem isn't Lisbet. It's getting off this island. Right now that doesn't look too hopeful. I guess we're darned lucky this is a warm night."

Courtney looked down at her brief swimsuit, then at Link's, and burst into peals of laughter. They were hardly dressed for an extended visit, and of all the people she would choose to be marooned on an island with, her lawyer-partner-landlord wouldn't be first choice.

"You're not going to get hysterical on me, are you?" He moved toward her as though he might have to take her in hand.

She took a step backward, gulped, and regained her composure. "Me, hysterical? Never. Cool as a cucumber in a crisis, that's Courtney James." Then, remembering Georgie's short conversation with Link before they'd taken Andy on the water, she said, sweetly, "I hope you didn't have plans for this evening."

"I didn't. But Georgie had some for me."

"Oh. Sorry and double sorry. She'll be furious."

"She'll survive. I'll have some explaining to do." To the judge, too, probably, he thought. "She won't like it, but she'll live." He sighed, splashed over the side and held out his hand to help Courtney from the boat. "It's really getting dark. Come on. We may as well stay dry."

"Wait. There should be a blanket in this compartment under the cushions," Courtney said. "And there should be a kit in here with a couple of flares, too, and a flashlight. Hopefully, some mosquito repellant, as well." She rummaged in a set of double doors under the seat. The flashlight was there, but the batteries gave off only enough light to reveal that the flares were missing.

"The flares are gone!" Courtney cried indignantly. "How rotten! And to think that someone I rented to would have stooped so low as to steal survival equipment!" She picked up the blanket, and they waded back toward shore to re-secure the line.

"Hmmm." He grinned. "Speaking of survival, it's too bad you didn't have some Colonel Sanders chicken or a sandwich or two stashed away in there."

Courtney groaned. "Don't even mention food. I was famished before but now I'm really starving. Let's find a good spot to watch for a late-returning boat. Maybe we can hitch a ride."

It was almost completely dark now except for a low streak of light against the horizon, and there wasn't a glimmer of anything moving anywhere on the bay. It looks as though we're in for a long night, Courtney thought as they sloshed to shore. A long night.

"You wouldn't happen to have any matches, would you?" She followed his amused glance down to his brief black swimsuit and realized how ridiculous her question was. "I guess not."

His lithe body stood out clearly from the darkening trees behind him. With his broad shoulders and perfect proportions, and except for the modern swimsuit he wore, Lincoln Spencer could have passed for displaced marble statue of an ancient Greek. He silently reached out to take her hand, and once again she felt that unexpected sparkle, a kind of electricity that tingled through her, bringing each nerve alive, warming her whole being.

This was no statue. This was a flesh and blood man.

The man my sister has her sights set on, Courtney reminded herself wryly. It's too bad we can't exchange places.

Chapter Twelve

"I don't suppose you're much good at rubbing two sticks together?" Courtney asked hopefully as they stood again on the small cleared space where they'd sat to watch the sunset. Stars began to fill the cloudless sky with myriad twinkling specks. There was no moon, but as each star came into view its watery counterpart reflected double brilliance from the quiet water into the warm summer night.

"Sorry about that," Lincoln shook his head. "I don't suppose you are, either."

"No such luck. I have some other virtues, though, in case you're wondering."

"Oh? Sounds interesting."

Her face was a perfect pale oval against the dark trees. "Well, I'm patient, when I have to be. I'm truly not bad company, usually. I'm not allergic to mosquitoes, and that may be important on a night like this. And I don't cry over spilt milk. Or, in this case, spilt gasoline."

"Whew. That's quite a list." His smile was barely discernable in the dusk. "I take it, then, that you subscribe to the old saying about accepting what you can't change?"

She sensed his intent to keep things light, and laughed. "I guess. Something about when you don't have a choice, relax and enjoy?"

"That's the one."

They spread the large beach towel back on approximately the same place it had been earlier and piled the boat cushions on it.

"Well. Know any good games to play in the dark?" Courtney asked flippantly as they sat down, but her voice had a give-away tremor. What was she doing here and how was she going to handle this situation? Lincoln's nearness was disturbing, and her body was uncomfortably warm from the inside out, doing things that she didn't expect, and didn't want. She felt a monumental physical attraction to this man that she'd never felt before, even with Ronnie. In spite of their earlier companionship, this was a potentially explosive situation and being here for an entire night was definitely not part of any program she'd planned.

"Games like what? Twenty Questions? Sports Trivia?"

"Or something."

He was quiet for a few moments as they watched dozens, then suddenly, as darkness descended in earnest, hundreds more stars appear from black space to dot the sky from horizon to zenith. "I was always too busy to bother with trivial pursuits, I guess," Link admitted. "I couldn't tell you who was on the old radio shows, or who batted what in the 1937 World Series. Sorry. Any other suggestions?"

"What were you too busy with?" That seemed a safe enough subject, Courtney thought, and since the night was going to be long for sure, any kind of conversation would help.

"Learning law. And political science."

"You're going into politics?"

"I'd like to, eventually." Remembering his fishing conversation—fishing in more ways than one—with Judge Burns, Link made a face in the dark. Would being part of the Judge's corporation interfere with his own hopes to move into politics? Was it an assurance of the support of Judge Burns' influential *party men*? Or, was it a means of being manipulated by the judge for his own ends? And did a political future in Illinois really depend on his marrying Georgie? Right this minute, he could barely remember her face. With surprise he realized that, although it was too dark to discern Courtney's features, he could picture everything about her without even trying.

"Real politics? State office, you mean?"

"Yes, probably."

"You mean Illinois."

"I thought so, until just recently. As a matter of fact, Wisconsin's a great state but there are some things that I feel I could improve, if I had the chance, and some clout. I think I might like to move my practice back here and give it a try."

His words were a surprise even to himself. But here he wouldn't need the judge's backing. Actually, it wouldn't carry much weight in Door County. The people's lifelong knowledge of Uncle Tom, Aunt Amy and himself would be more important here. It was certainly an avenue worth thinking about. He brought his mind back to their conversation. "And how about you, Miss Courtney?"

His low, resonant voice seemed even more so in the warm starlight night, and an answering shiver ran through her body. "Me?"

"You. Courtney James, Proprietor. What are her dreams, aspirations, plans for the Capital F Future?"

"I guess I'm more concerned with the present," said Courtney slowly. "I love it here and I want to make a go of the store, for now, more than anything. It's important to me to be successful at it with whatever future that implies, my first venture into business for myself, and all that. But do I want to run a sports store all my life? Right now, yes. Maybe not. I'm moving away from my past more than into my capital F future right now, I guess..." Her voice trailed off as she realized what she'd said, and that it was the truth. She was still moving away from Ronnie, still grieving, and that had gone on too long. It was time to plan ahead. But for what?

"You're very quiet," he said, finally.

"Sorry. Lost in the past, I guess." She changed the subject. "Have you been to see the Peninsula Players yet this summer?"

"Not yet. But I will. Georgie's hot on seeing the oldest repertory group in the country, she says. I'm not sure she knows what that means."

A few lights dotted the horizon but nothing was close enough to contribute in any way to a rescue, and the water and sky became a velvet quilt tied by stars as they talked about anything and everything—their childhoods, parents, likes and dislikes, plays they'd seen, music they loved. He was interested in everything about her, and before she realized it, Courtney found herself revealing more about her life with Ronnie and her bitterness about the racing world than she intended.

"But you have to admit, it is exciting," he said. He'd felt that excitement many times, watching. Not wishing he were part of it, exactly, but reveling in the race, the chance, the win.

"No doubt about that. Too much so, for me."

"From what I observed, Mitchell would like to bring you back to it."

"Jerry?" She considered. "No. He knows how I feel."

"What about Lisbet?"

Courtney felt a tug somewhere inside at the mention of her sister and realized she had totally forgotten Lisbet and her own *you can have him* promise about the man beside her. "What do you mean? What about her?"

"Does she feel the way you do about racing?"

"I don't think so. Not to the same extent, surely.

Why do you ask?"

"Oh, just wondered. Tell me about Andy."

Safe ground. "Little Andy. Isn't he a sweetheart?" Courtney's voice warmed. "Lisbet doesn't know how lucky she is to have him. I'm so glad he's getting healthier. He's asthmatic sometimes, you know, and has panic attacks. He was sick so often last year, after her divorce." Courtney wrapped her arms around her legs and leaned her chin on her knees. "We have an ESP game, he and I." She told Link about the hours she and her sister had spent playing "Where am I hiding?" when Lisbet had been sick, and how much Andy enjoyed the game. "He delights in outwitting me. He keeps coming up with places I couldn't dream of, getting wilder and wilder. Yesterday it was some imaginary cave up the cliff behind the cottages." She smiled, remembering Andy's joy in winning. "I told him he was cheating, it had to be a real place. He just giggled." She grew serious. "I wanted a son. I suppose everyone does."

"It's not too late."

"Sure. Maybe I could mail-order one from J.C. Penney's."

"Funny. I mean, you'll marry again, surely."

"Order up a husband, too, probably. Bigger than life. Dark, with a good physique." She stopped, realizing that she was describing the swimsuited man seated beside her.

"Hopefully with enough money to live comfortably and buy bonbons for your novel-reading hours." His tone was light and teasing, and the awkward moment was gone.

Only three hours had passed, though it seemed much longer, before he asked, "Tired?"

"Not really. Not sleepy-tired, anyway. How about you?"

"Wide awake."

His nearness was comforting; at the same time it was disturbing. She felt betrayed by a body that remembered his touch as he'd lifted her from the boat, that ached to be held close to that muscled chest, to feel those strong arms around her. Courtney deliberately closed her eyes against the starlight, but opened them immediately. The night was too spectacular to shut away. There was a luminous quality about it that made everything seem softly lit, and suddenly a blue flicker shot up from the horizon on the far side of the bay.

"Oh! What's that? Lightning? Don't tell me we have a summer storm coming up!" There was no shelter here on this little patch of wilderness in the bay.

"Not a chance," chuckled Link. "That's the aurora borealis. Northern lights. You've never seen them before?"

"Never! I have heard about them, though. You're not likely to see them above Milwaukee's bright lights. This is exciting!" Courtney hugged her knees in anticipation, looking like a small child at Christmas. "Will they be bigger? Higher, I mean? Are they colored?"

"Sometimes. It depends. I've seen them cover the sky from the horizon to the very top. Spectacular. And," he pointed to another section of the horizon where more streaks began to shimmer upwards, "it looks as though that might be the program tonight. In special honor of Courtney James, who's never seen them before."

Breathless, Courtney stared at the flickering, changing yellow-greens, blues and sometimes even reds that streamed up from the horizon, flowing out of the earth to ripple up through the sky, streaming toward the zenith in an ever-changing, electrical panorama.

"It's beautiful," she whispered. "It hides the

stars for seconds at a time. It reflects in the water until the whole world is changing, shimmering—oh, it's-it's—" Her voice broke and surprising tears filled her eyes. She brushed them away. "I don't know what to say."

"I know. It affects me like that, too. Say nothing. Just be. Enjoy." Lincoln Spencer's velvet voice, so close to her ear, enveloped Courtney, as did the warm summer night, the northern lights; the enormity of the spectacular world surrounding them. There was light enough for her to look up into the intense grey eyes so close to her own.

She was drowning in those eyes, in this magic night.

"Courtney." His arms came around her and his finger lifted her chin to bring her full, parted lips so close to his that his warm breath mingled with hers as he murmured again, "Just be. Enjoy." And then his kiss claimed her.

A moment out of time lifted Courtney to a plane of sensuous longing and her mouth invited his to search hers, first gently and tenderly, feather-brushing her lips, then probing, more demanding. His warm fingers played her senses as he caressed the back, slipping under and over and around the frail strap of her bikini bra.

His lips found her throat, the small hollow that revealed the pounding of her heart, and as he moved his mouth again to hers, her body moved against him and invited his teasing, tantalizing tongue and hands. Her arms slid easily around his back, her fingers threading through the thick dark hair at the nape of his neck.

Courtney was aware of her shoulders being lowered gently but firmly to the boat cushions as Link's other hand traced the line of her throat, her shoulder, slowly, so slowly down her side to the warm curve of her hip above her brief suit. His palm

was hot against her skin and gently stroked away
any resistance to his desire.

Her mind swirled, out of control; her pulse
pounded as her tongue eagerly accepted his and
asked for more, more. Her back arched to push her
heated breasts toward his furred, bare chest. She
willed him to loosen her bra, and when he did she
pulled her hands free from around his neck to cup
her breasts and offer them to his hunger.

He moaned softly as he nuzzled her full breasts,
nipping them gently to desiring peaks, then
relieving them with a slow manipulation of his
sensitive lips as he whispered her name over and
over. Her body responded to his expert hands and
mouth as though she were born to be his lover, and
he slowly slid his knee between her thighs.

"Yes, yes," she whispered, her body
remembering, wanting, aching for the fulfillment
that would come, her hips arching toward his body
above her as he slipped her bikini briefs off with a
slow movement, then ran his palm down her flat
belly to her tangled softness. Courtney heard herself
making small noises that made no sense but fell
away into the summer night as though they were
part of it.

"Courtney, Courtney," Link whispered. "You do
want me, don't you?" he murmured softly. She
pressed her fingers down his muscled back, sliding
them into the waistband of his skin-tight suit. Her
whole body shuddered as with one swift movement
he stood above her and stripped; in the flickering
northern lights he became a sensuous, mythical god
of fertility.

Wide-eyed, her back arched in anticipation, her
body a burning vessel of desire, Courtney caught her
breath as he lowered himself to her, as he slowly ran
his hands over and around her breasts, kneading
them in slow movements that pulled her toward

him, then running his palms down her sides, over her stomach, moving ever so slowly down her thighs, spreading her knees gently, gently.

She could stand it no longer. "Now! Please!" Her hands pulled him down, down, upon and into her, her body moved with him as he thrust, torching her desire into a hot flame that burned to be fed, that remembered and needed and surrendered, giving as much pleasure as she received. Rejoicing in the thrill of his hard body united with hers, she moved with the universe as the northern lights rose and fell behind his head above her and his breath was warm and fierce on her face.

There was no island, no earth, no past, no future. Aware of nothing but their passion, Courtney soared into the infinite with every fiber of her being, as together, slowly at first, then faster and faster, with sounds that mixed with this night, this moment, they rose together into the zenith as the sky exploded above them.

Spent in the aftermath, Courtney drifted into a warm sleep, her head pillowed on his chest, her lips tasting his salty sweat. She opened her eyes once to see that the northern lights had diminished and again there were only stars, above and reflected in the quiet waters of the bay. You could swim through those stars, she thought drowsily; maybe I already have.

Content, blanketed against the night chill as Link's warmth mingled with hers, Courtney sighed and snuggled, molding her body to his. She murmured something just before she fell asleep, but in the morning she was unable to remember just what it had been.

Chapter Thirteen

In the soft mist-light of early dawn a loon's cry echoed eerily across the water and Courtney woke to find Lincoln Spencer leaning on one elbow above her, his grey eyes studying her face intently. Behind him the trees were dark silhouettes fading into the brightening sky.

"Oh," she said inadequately, flushing as he shifted the blanket and his roving eyes followed the curve of her bare breasts, stopped momentarily, then traveled her flat belly and continued down to her inner thighs before he looked up into her face.

"Good morning," he said.

He sounded...wary? She caught her lower lip between her teeth. Did he think she was going to come off as the wronged woman, or what? Courtney looked away from his grey stare, hanging somewhere between embarrassment for her lusty acceptance of him in the electrified dark of the romantic night and the unwelcome thought at the sight of his nude body that she probably would find it very difficult to refuse if he wanted to begin it all again. Would he?

She gave her head a little shake, reminding herself again that this man that Courtney had freely given herself to, was the man Lisbet had her heart set on.

She scrambled to a sitting position, her tangled hair tumbling in wavy ropes around her shoulders, her face becomingly pink. "I don't...you must think...that is...I'm not...don't want you to think..." her voice trailed off.

He smiled, his eyes crinkling into small crows' feet at the corners, and there was that annoying underlying amusement in his voice. "I won't if you won't."

"We were simply victims of circumstance," Courtney said quickly, kneeling to search the sand for her swimsuit, trying not to look at him as he uncurled himself and stood, totally unselfconscious in his nude state, above her. It was hard to keep her eyes from him. He was physically magnificent. And, she realized, flushing, most obviously capable of taking advantage of their lonely circumstances again.

"Oh?" He raised his heavy brows. "Nothing more?"

"Nothing more." There, she'd said it. And she had found her bra. Now, where was the bottom half of that elusive suit?

"Right. Of course. Biology just took over." His tone held irony. There had been a whole lot more, at least on her part, and she knew he knew it.

Courtney felt her face redden again. "There'll be boats as soon as it's light enough to fish." She pulled her brief bikini bottom from under the edge of the rumpled blanket and shook it energetically to remove the sand.

"Well, then. We'd better dress, such as it is, hadn't we?"

That struck a funny note, and in spite of herself Courtney laughed, holding up the two minuscule parts of her suit. "Won't take long, will it? It's about getting the sand out, first."

Spencer threw back his head and laughed, too, an easy, tension-easing laugh, and held out his hand to pull her up. "A daybreak swim will take care of that. Come on."

It seemed foolish to feel anything but free and happy, and laughing, hand in hand, carrying their sandy suits, they ran into the cool morning water, washing away the night, the stars, and the magical northern lights.

An hour later, towed by a luckily non-verbal early morning fisherman, they quietly docked the ski boat at Courtney's pier.

"I feel like a teenager sneaking home after a too-late night," Courtney confided as they walked stealthily up the path to where it split to each of their cottages. "I'm glad it's still so early." In the quiet morning air even their whispers seemed to carry.

As they parted, Link caught her hands for just a moment and looked deep into her eyes. "Courtney. Do you remember what you said to me last night just before you fell asleep?"

"No." She bit her lower lip. "Am I sorry?"

"I hope not." He grinned. "But I won't hold you to it."

Puzzled, she watched him walk up to his porch, his lithe, athletic form moving steadily and surely on the uneven, root-rough ground. He didn't appear to suffer from the stiffness that seemed determined to settle into her body from their night on unforgiving ground. As she turned and walked slowly toward her own cottage, she realized with a shock that not once during their passion, or even during the rest of their time together, had she thought of Ronnie.

Some therapy, she mused, smiling. She felt wonderful. Maybe it was time for her to break away from the past and start thinking about the Capital F future, as Link had put it.

Later, Courtney hummed as she straightened shelves and reminded herself to reprimand Bobby for not filling the gas tank on the ski boat. What if a customer had been stranded? That could have created an uncomfortable situation all around. Perhaps even an unwelcome and expensive lawsuit.

The door chimes announced Lisbet. "Boy, you must have been late last night," she said. "I waited around for a while but gave it up and took Andy home. Did you stop for dinner someplace, or what?"

Courtney busied herself at a low shelf, not meeting Lisbet's questioning eyes. "How'd you guess? As a matter of fact, we picked up a couple of hamburgers at some waterfront place up the way that Link remembered from his misspent youth." She would have to remember to ask him to back her up. Last night was a closed chapter that she wasn't about to repeat, and there was no way in the world she was going to admit to Lisbet what really happened. Or how she felt about it. And that, she thought, I don't really know.

"Hope you enjoyed yourself. I'd have loved to have a hamburger, or anything else, with that one." Lisbet sighed. "And I'll bet the sunset was even more beautiful out away from shore."

It was, thought Courtney. The whole night was beautiful, from the sunset to the northern lights, from the friendship to the passion, and even to the morning swim. She pulled her thoughts to the present as Lisbet spoke.

"Oh, by the way, Bobby won't be here until afternoon. He stopped by last night to tell you. Said he filled all the boats yesterday before he left and they should be good until noon."

"Really!" Courtney's head came up swiftly. "Are you sure?"

"That's what he said. Why?"

"Oh...nothing, really..." Courtney caught her breath at a sudden surge of anger. Had Lincoln Spencer pulled a fast one on her? Was there actually gas in the tank after all? She hadn't checked for herself, and he had filled the tank this morning when they got back. Was it possible that he'd contrived to stall them on that island on purpose?

What a sophomoric thing to do!

Courtney closed her eyes, remembering Link's guileless expression as he told her the tank was empty, and seeing again the flickering sky behind his dark head as their passion rose. Had the island, the night, the magical wonder of it all—had that all been nothing more than a macho scheme to prove something on his part?

And had she fallen for it!

Courtney slapped a package of lead sinkers down on a shelf. "Hold the fort a few minutes, will you, Liss?" she asked, trying to sound natural though her voice was nearly choked to a squawk. "I forgot something."

"Sure." Lisbet, apparently not noticing anything unusual, plunked down on the stool behind the cash register, and Courtney made herself walk slowly out the door and to the corner of the store before she gave way to her suspicions.

Then she charged full speed up the path to Link's cabin, laying muttered but explicit curses on Lincoln Spencer with each furious step. She'd bang on that door until it fell in if she had to. She'd show that arrogant city lawyer a thing or three. He'd better have a damn good explanation for that supposed empty tank, or else.

But there was no answer to her knocks. The closed inner cabin door appeared to be locked but she tried the screen, and as she opened it a piece of paper fluttered to the ground. It was not addressed to anyone in particular, and Courtney unfolded it to read, "Called away. Complications. Back when I can. Link."

She stuffed the note back between the doors and slammed the screen so hard a dozen pine cones rattled off the roof and skittered down the path. Called away, was he? Not likely. Ran was more like it, she'd bet. Why oh why had she ever trusted

Lincoln Spencer? Obviously her first impression of him had been right.

Fuming futilely, Courtney breathed deeply to calm herself as she walked slowly down to the store. Damn the man! Seething, she noticed a long, dawn-grey Cadillac parked next to the building.

Not my usual clientele, she thought, probably someone looking for our friend Spencer. If it was, she'd like to tell them where they could go to find him, and it wouldn't be any place particularly comfortable.

As she rounded the corner of the store she was caught in a monstrous, unexpected bear hug and nearly smothered by a hearty kiss that cut off her startled exclamation.

"Logan Andrews!" she gasped as soon as she could catch her breath. "Whatever in the world are you doing up here? You've almost crushed the life out of me!" Relieved not to have to explain her hurried departure up the hill to Lisbet, or her obvious anger on return, she welcomed the distraction of Logan Andrews with open arms and led him inside the store.

"Mind introducing me, Court?" asked Lisbet, who had watched their effusive greeting through the window. "Friend of yours, I take it?"

"More than a friend. Logan, meet my sister Lisbet. Logan Andrews."

"Your old boss!" Lisbet held out a hand. "Well, obviously not so old! I've heard so much about you I almost think I should have recognized you."

Logan raised his well-trimmed eyebrows at Courtney.

"Only the best," she said quickly. "Right, Liss? Now, answer my question, Logan. What brings you here?"

Logan, impeccably dressed as always in an expensive suit that matched his graying temples, with complimentary tie and shoes polished to a gleaming shine, seemed totally out of place between fishing lures and life jackets. He stepped back to take a good look at Courtney, and seemed to like what he saw. "Coming to find you, my pet. What else?"

"Sure you were," she said, smiling. "Uh-huh. Now tell the truth."

"I just happened to be in the neighborhood?"

"Won't do."

He tapped a long cigarette on a gold case as he asked, "Tell me, do you miss your old haunts? Or do you enjoy going to work in denims and plaids instead of suits and heels?"

She glanced down at her trim jeans and grinned. "Matter of fact, yes. To both questions. Depends on the circumstances, the time of day, and the kind of customers I'm having. Logan, it's wonderful to see you, really it is." Courtney pulled out a folding chair from behind the counter. "Sit down and tell me all the gossip at Ladd's."

"That won't take long. It's been dull without you."

"I'll bet." Courtney laughed. "You old fake. I know you didn't drive all the way here just to declare that you miss me, or to get a view of my store, though you have to admit, don't you, that it's much better than you thought? Now, 'fess up. What's going on?"

"First, let me assure you that your store is truly much grander than I thought. I'm impressed. But in answer to what brings me here, there are two things, really." Logan looked around for an ash try, and Courtney handed him one fashioned like a frog from the counter. "And, looking over your inventory, I can see that it's lucky I stopped. More than lucky, fortuitous. For you."

"Really." Courtney made a face at him. "I could

use a little fortuitousness right about now. Tell on."

"I'm on my way to a management conference up on Washington Island for three days. Then, at the end of this week, I'm going down to Chicago to take in the International Sporting Clothing Exhibition." He looked from Courtney to Lisbet as he spoke. "Aha! I see I have whetted your interest."

"That sounds fascinating," said Lisbet, leaning her elbows on the checkout counter. "Courtney's been talking about getting in a line of women's sporting clothes, haven't you, Court?"

Courtney nodded. "We need something to attract the women who aren't all that interested in angling, for sure. Go on, Logan."

"Well, I thought I'd stop here on my way up, convince you that you must come on down to the buyers' show, and spirit you away for some weekend fun and games in the big city. How about it?"

Courtney hesitated, but Lisbet bubbled, "That would be great for you, Court!" She stepped around the checkout counter. "You've been working far too hard, and you need a break. Everything's running fine here and I can handle the place with Bobby's help. Anyway, remember? Jerry's coming up for the weekend and he'll give me a hand if I need it." She nodded vigorously at Courtney. "It's the perfect opportunity for you to pick up the clothes you want to fill in with the tackle and ski stuff. Winter cross-country and next season's summer wear. Go for it!"

Logan agreed, standing to put a friendly arm around Lisbet's shoulders. "I like this sister of yours, Courtney. She's all right! Good head on this one."

Lisbet grinned up at him.

"It's a conspiracy," Courtney grumbled, looking from one to the other, but her hesitation was only momentary. Getting away from Sister Bay right now and getting her mind on something other than Lincoln Spencer's devious chicanery sounded like a terrific idea.

"Why not?" she said, nodding. "I can catch a bus back on Sunday, or Monday morning. I'll do it. Logan, you're wonderful."

"I know," he said, winking at Lisbet. "It's my nature." They all laughed.

"Give me ten minutes' notice to get out of my working duds and into something spiffy when you come back, and Chicago, here I come!" Courtney turned to Lisbet, "You're sure, Liss? You won't mind? I can't close the store."

"Absolutely. I'll feel needed, for a change, not just an extra. Envious, though. So you better enjoy."

Enjoy. That was what Lincoln Spencer said last night. Relax and enjoy. Courtney pulled her thoughts from his deceit. "See you Friday, then, Logan." Courtney walked him to his car. "Neat wheels," she said, appraising his automobile with approval.

He patted the shiny hood. "It matches my suit."

"Doesn't everything?" she countered.

He grinned. "See you Friday. About six."

Chapter Fourteen

This is just what she needed, Courtney decided as she and Logan drove over the high bridge at Sturgeon Bay. The harbor below was dotted with tethered sailboats and the sun on the water was as bright as she felt. Dressed in what Lisbet described as *driving to the city* clothes, a pair of beige sharkskin slacks and matching blouse with a pale blue sweater over her shoulders, Courtney leaned back in the seat, relieved to have a two-day respite from fishhooks and worm boxes, sputtering motors and mostly overweight, affluent tourists who complained about everything. If the weather was good, the fish didn't bite. If the fish bit, it was either too hot or too cold or too windy. If the weather and the fish were both perfect, the mosquitoes were terrible. She flipped her hair up over the seat back, shut her eyes and let out a long breath.

"Whew! That was a big sigh," Logan observed. "Want to talk about it?"

"Not a whole lot to talk about. It's just a relief to get away from the store."

Logan raised his eyebrows. "Shall I say I told you so?"

"No, silly. It's really going fine. I'm just tired. Lisbet was right. I can really use this get-away."

Courtney lazily stretched her long legs as she watched the miles slide past. The scenic road they were on would keep Lake Michigan in sight at least part of the way down to the city. Logan appeared at ten and she and her small suitcase had been installed in his Cadillac not more than fifteen minutes later.

Courtney put a hand over his on the wheel. "Did I say thank you, Logan? You're like a breath of fresh air after some of the people I've been dealing with lately."

"Tourists tough to please?"

"You said it."

"Forget them."

"I'd like to, mostly." She smiled. "But not always, of course." And, she thought, there was someone else she'd like to forget, too, but that wasn't as easy. She kept remembering Lincoln Spencer's smoldering eyes, his so tender yet demanding hands, his body silhouetted against the trees and pressing itself to hers. The memory was not unpleasant...if only he hadn't tricked her into it. And then disappeared when she would have confronted him.

Logan shifted comfortably in the driver's seat and pulled out a slim cigarette. "Smoke?" At the shake of her head, he lit up from a thin gold lighter, inhaled deeply, and said, "You know, these cruise controls are wonderful. I can devote nearly all my attention to my beautiful passenger."

"Really!" Courtney laughed, then sobered. "I've missed your flirting, Logan."

"Who's flirting? I'm just being honest. Now you be honest with me, and tell me that you've been desolately lonely for good food, good companionship and cultural advancement."

Courtney studied his face. Was he teasing? She decided not. His carefully combed light brown hair, now more silver at the temples than she remembered, was, as usual, perfectly in place. His mustache matched his hair so well she was almost sure they both had to be colored to the same perfect shade. His grey and maroon-striped silk tie was knotted just right, his fingernails short but buffed to a dull sheen. All in all, he was a man any woman would be proud to be seen with. Why didn't she want him? More than once he'd declared himself available, ready and willing. She wondered if that was a problem she might have to deal with later tonight.

Logan's reputation as a womanizer wasn't lost on any of the females who worked with him. His social calendar was as busy, or busier, than the one on his desk. Courtney had spent many pleasant evenings with him: plays at the Pabst Theatre, art openings at the museum, evenings at the symphony. Warm times, but not passionate ones, due to her reluctance, not his often-stated wishes. She could have had an affair with Logan, but she would be one of many. No, thanks. When—or if—she loved again, it would be a mature give and take. Not the *out of gas, guess we'll have to be together all night* sort of fling she'd just experienced. Even the thought of that, and Lincoln Spencer, made her furious. No, she wanted a forever thing, if there was such a thing any more. Circumstances had taken that away from her and Ronnie.

She and Logan had talked about Door County before she'd pulled up stakes and headed north. He'd been wrong about winter in Door being a wasteland. She'd spent enough weekends at her cottage during the last cold months to know and enjoy the County's serene, snow-covered personality as well as its exciting summer season.

She brought her mind back to his question. "Well, to be honest, I haven't lacked for good food because, believe it or not, I'm not a bad cook, and neither is my sister. Companionship comes and goes, some good..." she thought of Jerry Mitchell, "and some not so good." Her mind flew back again to the wonderful, deceitful night on Sisters Island.

"And?"

She smiled. "And I'm holding up quite well,

thank you. As for culture, I haven't had much time for it yet but the Peninsula Players—they're the oldest summer stock theater in the whole country, by the way, did you know that?—are excellent. I'm told that most of their plays are successes from Broadway. They're nearly always sold out. And the art galleries..."

She stopped as Logan held up a hand in protest. "Whoa! Hold up! I didn't ask for a brochure from the Chamber of Commerce, for heaven's sake! You're ignoring the meat of my question. What about male company?" There was a wistful note in his voice.

"Don't ask. What I've met has left something to be desired." Was that a Freudian slip? Did she desire Lincoln Spencer? "But other than that, life is good. I love the county, and most of the people I've met have been great. So that's all there is about me. What about you?"

The miles passed companionably as they discussed the young male replacement who had taken her position at Ladd's, the latest plays at the Pabst Theatre and who Logan had been with to see them, and the new developments in both their lives.

"You know you're welcome back any time you want to come, Courtney. There will always be a place for you as long as I'm head buyer for Ladd's."

Courtney reached over and covered his hand with hers. "Thanks, Logan. I appreciate knowing that. It will keep me going when the weather is bad and nobody wants anything from Courtney's Sports. But so far, no thanks. I'm pleased with what I've accomplished, and proud of how it's turning out." She paused. "I really had been thinking of putting in at least some women's apparel in the store, so I'm not coming with you under false pretenses."

"You can come under any pretenses you want, I don't care," he declared, smiling. "I really have missed you. Oh, I'm not staying home night after night, you know that, but we had some good times, didn't we?"

Courtney nodded. "That we certainly have. You don't need to talk as if we'll never have them again."

Logan glanced at her. "I wonder. You've changed, you know."

"The inevitable. Age."

"No, something else. Something indescribable. As if, oh...I don't know, as if your life is more fulfilling, or something. I worried about you after Ronnie died. You carried such an empty look sometimes. And now, if anything, you're more beautiful than ever."

Courtney felt herself flush with pleasure. "Words to cheer a woman to her very soul." But she did feel different. More competent, perhaps, more sure of herself. "Come on, let's change the subject. Tell me about what we're going to do in Chicago."

Logan deftly passed a semi-truck before answering. "Here's the plan, if it meets your approval, Miz James. We'll stop somewhere on the way down for a midday meal. I know a couple of nice places in good old Milwaukee, remember, and I'll drop you at the Hyatt when we get to Chicago. Your room is reserved. You'll have the evening to yourself, I'm sorry to say. I have to meet with someone. But tomorrow morning I'll pick you up and take you to the show."

"Where is it held?"

"The usual. McCormick Place."

Courtney was quiet for a moment, picturing the building as she remembered it from previous buying sprees for Ladd's. "Do you know, I've never been in Chicago overnight before? That seems funny, with all the trips I made there for the company. But it was always close enough to get back easily to my Milwaukee apartment."

"Really! Then we'll have to do the town. Plan on

it. My day time is going to be more taken up than I'd like, I'm afraid. I have a couple of people to meet with both morning and afternoon, and I definitely want to take in some of the show, but I'll meet you at the second floor lobby for cocktails at six before I take you to dinner tomorrow night. Okay?"

"Oh, Logan. I don't want to take your time from clients."

"Foolish lady. Look in the glove compartment, will you?"

"What for?"

"Just do."

Puzzled, she opened the compartment and found a plastic card that had her name imprinted on it as Owner-buyer for Courtney's Sports, Sister Bay, Wisconsin. "Where in the world did you get this?" she gasped.

"Just like magic: you need a pass to get in, so I had one made."

"You weren't certain I'd come, or anything, were you?" she accused, laughing.

"I could only hope."

"Oh, Logan, thanks. I feel pampered." She slipped the badge into her purse.

"As you should." He smiled. "It's my pleasure to pamper beautiful women."

"You'll never change." She looked out the window at the green Wisconsin countryside sliding by. "And right now, I'm glad. I could use a little pampering."

He sent her a sideways questioning look. "More than you can handle up there in good old Door County? Your store looks fine. Small, but compact and you have a lot in it. And you said you were busy enough."

"I'm really tired. Mind if I nap?"

"In other words, subject closed. Take your nap. We'll talk later." He turned his attention to the road.

The next morning Courtney was up early, well rested and excited about the show, which opened at nine. As she dressed in a bone-white summer suit with a dusty rose silk blouse that enhanced her tanned complexion, she thought about the day and evening to come. Though their rooms were on the same floor, she hadn't seen Logan after checking in last night, and, to be honest, she'd been relieved. Tonight, however, might be a different story.

Courtney finished twisting her hair into an elegant upsweep and smiled as she put a finishing touch to her makeup—she'd almost forgotten how to put it on—and slipped her soft rose lipstick into her bone-white leather shoulder bag. She felt excited to be back in the city, dressed for business right down to her stylish pumps. It seemed as though Sister Bay and Sisters Island were a world away.

That night on the island had revived a lot of things she had put aside from her life, most and forefront sensual and, she had to admit, most enjoyable, sex. She had missed that terribly. Suddenly there were a lot of new-old feelings swirling through her body, and she didn't quite know what to make of them. She wondered whether Logan, experienced lover that she felt sure he would be, would have brought out the same feelings as Lincoln Spencer.

Forget him, Courtney told herself as she pulled her hotel door closed behind her. You're here in Chicago, you have an exciting show to see, clothes to buy for Courtney's Sports, and an entertaining evening ahead. She smiled to herself as she stepped into the elevator. It was exhilarating to be back in what someone like Miss Georgie Burns would call *civilization*.

Logan smiled broadly as Courtney walked toward him across the lobby. "You haven't lost your classy touch in dressing, have you? That suit is marvelous. Just the thing to make all these clothing people realize they're dealing with a pro. Come on, my love, the sporting world awaits your return."

Courtney laughed and took his proffered arm. Door County and Courtney's Sports, with its problems—and pleasures—seemed very far away indeed.

Chapter Fifteen

Hours later, exhausted from viewing booth after booth of sports goods for every activity and clothing from dozens of countries, Courtney sank down on a comfortable chair on the second floor of McCormick Place. She pulled off her high heels and rubbed her nyloned feet that had hardly worn anything but tennies or boat shoes for the past months.

Her day had been exhilarating, although—she grimaced—she had probably overextended her credit. Sports fashions were fun, especially some of the things she'd ordered for next season, as well as for winter cross-country skiing. But she'd kept her eyes open and knew what both tourists and natives would buy in Sister Bay.

She leaned back and closed her eyes, thanking heaven for small favors. At least there was nothing in her contract with Amy Lane about needing permission to stock what was necessary to upgrade the store.

Amy.

Courtney closed her eyes and pictured the kindly sweet-faced lady and wondered for the hundredth time why, in all their talks about their contract, the fact that Lincoln Spencer had considered doing the same had never been mentioned. Perhaps the dear old lady hadn't taken him seriously, a successful lawyer miles away. Probably he had seemed to be humoring her since that was how her husband Tom had used the property. Evidently Lincoln had worshiped Tom.

There must have been a reason, but it wasn't a puzzle to which she was likely to learn the answer. She hoped Lincoln wouldn't impose his advice about her new inventory.

"There you are!"

She opened her eyes to see Logan standing above her, immaculate as always. "Put your shoes on, country girl, and we'll have a drink. Are you still fond of gimlets or have your tastes changed to something more plebeian? Maybe you're strictly a beer guzzler now?"

Courtney smiled up at him and grimaced as she slipped slowly into her confining pumps. "My tastes are still the same, Smarty. Believe it or not, you can buy vodka and Rose's lime even in little ol' Door County. A gimlet sounds divine. Have you finished with your appointments already?"

"Already! It's almost six. And no, I'm sorry to say, I have one more left." He held her elbow lightly as they made their way around knots of buyers heading in the same direction. "I'll have to see him yet tonight, unfortunately, as his plane leaves at ten. I am sorry. I'd hoped to squire you around to the bright lights and sights, since you said you'd never been here at night before." He steered her unerringly toward the bar set up at the end of the lobby. "But I have no choice. Dinner at The Palmer House? Or the restaurant at the Allerton? I hear it's been updated. Or do you hunger for something ethnic? Indian, or French? Your wish is my command."

Such a choice. After weeks of her own cooking or a quick sandwich at the grocery store checkout counter. Courtney thought for a moment. "Let's go back to the Palmer House. Remember the time we had lunch there and that funny little woman nearly fell all over you because you reminded her of her son?" Courtney grinned, remembering. "I thought I'd have to let her take you home!"

Logan smiled. "The one with the big paper bag. I always wondered what she had in it. It's funny now, but it was damn embarrassing at the time. She really was a screwy old thing, wasn't she? Followed us in right off the street."

A short time later, after a quick shower and new makeup, dressed for the evening in a shimmering turquoise cocktail dress that left her tanned arms and shoulders and most of her back bare, Courtney entered the familiar lobby of the Palmer Hotel on Logan's arm. She couldn't help glancing behind them.

"Looking for someone?" Logan inquired.

"Just little old ladies with brown paper shopping bags," she said, feeling a little foolish. "I'm sure there's no one within miles of here that I'd recognize."

Over their drinks and hors d'oeuvres they discussed various wholesale booths and some familiar people Courtney had caught up with. Over salad they talked about next year's swimsuit styles and leisure sports items, and, inevitably, over the main course of lobster and steak, they got around to themselves.

"It doesn't sound as though things have changed much for you, Logan."

"They haven't. And I wasn't fooling, I really do miss the things we shared, Court."

"There's no woman in your life?"

"I don't think there ever will be." He shrugged. "Maybe I'm just not cut out for the matrimonial brand of happiness."

Courtney caught the note of loneliness behind his words. "You just haven't met the right one yet, that's all."

"Or maybe you're it and neither of us knows it yet." He grinned engagingly and raised his glass to her. "Ever thought of that?"

Courtney's eyes widened in surprise. Was this a back-handed proposal? Or just another of Logan's continuous compliments? She opened her mouth, but her answer was lost as a high, familiar whine threaded through the room over the soft music and clink of dishes.

"And if you think you can keep shoving me off to that awful Sister Bay while you run back here and do interesting things—who with, I don't know—well, Mr. Lincoln Spencer, you can just forget it!"

Courtney gasped and turned, along with dozens of other diners around the room, to stare at the little blond who stood at a corner table, looking furiously down at a man wearing a tuxedo. Courtney felt a recognizable, unwelcome flush through her whole body at the sight of the handsome, well-dressed man and hoped it didn't show in her face.

Georgie Burns wore a floor-length gown of glittering green. Her light hair was piled in an elegant formal upsweep that didn't fit at all with the harsh belligerence in her voice. A white fur boa dripped from her shoulders.

Embarrassed, customers returned to their dinners and a busy hum of conversation covered whatever it was that Lincoln Spencer said calmly in return, though the deep color of his face belied that calmness.

"Hey! Hello! Over here, Courtney," Logan said, reaching across their table to touch her arm lightly. "Have you forgotten your manners? It's not polite to stare in public. From the expression on your face, I'd almost think you recognized that little blond bombshell."

Though she would have liked to deny any knowledge of Georgie Burns, Courtney said, "I do. But I certainly didn't expect to see her here." What in the world were Lincoln and Georgie doing here, and why, out of all the restaurants in downtown

Chicago, had Courtney chosen the one at the Palmer Hotel?

"Who is she?" Logan, in spite of his remark about staring, unabashedly followed the escalating scene across the room.

"You see before you Miss Georgie Burns," said Courtney, trying to keep the dislike from her voice. "She's been staying in Sister Bay with her father, for most of the summer, and very evidently against her wishes. She's a spoiled brat, if you want the truth."

Logan raised his eyebrows. "She looks like the kind it might be fun to spoil, though," he teased. "Look! She's going to pass right by our table."

"Wonderful." Courtney busied herself with her lobster. Maybe, with any luck, she wouldn't be noticed.

"And does she look furious!" Logan gaped openly as Georgie stomped toward them, trailing her white fur over one diamond-braceleted arm. As she came abreast of their table, she stopped short, stared at Courtney and stamped her high-heeled foot.

"You! Here! Ohhhh!"

Courtney winced at the venom in Georgie's voice but there was no need to answer as Georgie whipped the trailing fur around her shoulders with a toss of her chin and swept out the door.

Logan lifted his glass of champagne to Courtney's embarrassed, reddened face. "Well. There must be more to that story."

Uncomfortable under his scrutiny, Courtney looked down at her plate. Had Georgie somehow heard of their night on the island? Would a man who lied about an empty gas tank be above telling the story of his conquest? Oh, but surely not to his girl friend. Courtney twisted her napkin in her lap, unwilling to answer Logan. There was a whole lot more to the story, all right, but no one was going to hear it from her.

She was debating what to say to Logan, when a pair of elegantly trousered legs stopped beside her. Her gaze followed them up to meet Lincoln Spencer's grey eyes that seemed to envelop her, and her breath caught in her throat.

Why hadn't he gone on to follow his date and politely ignored Courtney and Logan? If there was anything she didn't need to be reminded of, it was this man and his deception on that night under northern lights.

"Miss James," Lincoln said formally, bowing slightly. "What a surprise!"

"Isn't it," she muttered, "I certainly didn't expect to run into anyone I knew here. Let alone you."

"Old friends?" asked Logan, looking from one to the other.

"Not exactly," said Courtney quickly, hating the color she knew had risen to her face. "Sorry, I'm forgetting my manners. Logan, this is Lincoln Spencer. Logan Andrews." She looked up at Spencer. "Forgive me for not asking you to join us," she said sweetly, "but your date is probably waiting for you."

"I doubt it," Link said easily. "She's most likely well away by cab already. When Miss Burns leaves, she leaves. And yes, thanks, I would love to join you." He smoothly pulled an unused chair from a nearby table and slid it next to hers. "May I?"

Logan, who had watched the tableau with interest, smiled benevolently and looked at his gold watch. "Please do. Actually, you're an answer to my prayer. Since your date has left, and since I have an appointment in a half hour at another hotel, you can do me a big favor by escorting Miss James back to the Hyatt when she's finished her drink. The little lady has had a long day."

"But Logan!" He couldn't just walk off and leave her! Her wide eyes pleaded with him, but he seemed unaware of the message she tried to convey. "You were going to show me the town!"

"I am sorry, Court. But it's unavoidable, as you know. Besides, it looks as though you'll be in very competent hands."

That's exactly what I'm afraid of, she thought, staring in disbelief as the two men shook hands and Logan left money on the table for the meal. "It's been wonderful being with you again, Courtney." Logan dropped a brief kiss on her forehead. "Will I see you in the morning?"

"No, I'm taking the early bus back to Sister Bay," she said, confused and miserable. How to get out of this without causing a scene?

"Oh. Right. Then next time. Let me know when you can make it to Milwaukee for a weekend." He turned to her companion. "Nice meeting you, Spencer. Take good care of our Courtney, will you? She's one of my favorite people."

Chapter Sixteen

With wide, unbelieving eyes, Courtney watched Logan's impeccably suited back disappear out the door of the restaurant. The nerve of him, to abandon her in the middle of Chicago. And to a man he'd only met a few minutes earlier!

She stared down into the clear, bubbling liquid in her glass until the silence grew unbearable, and she raised her eyes to the man seated near in the next chair. His smoky grey gaze was as disturbing as it had been when she'd awakened on the island in the half-light of dawn to find him staring down at her. That memory brought warm color flooding to her face and her whole body tingled.

"And am I the answer to your prayer, too, I hope?" he questioned.

"You! Hardly." She fixed him with a freezing aqua-blue gaze.

He lifted his heavy brows, puzzlement written all over his face. "Wait a minute! I thought we were friends, at last. Remember?"

"You lied," she accused, slapping her napkin down on the tabletop and pushing her chair back, preparing to walk out. "And I believed you. You must feel really pleased to have taken me in."

"What?" He frowned, shaking his head.

A great imitation of innocence, she thought. "The gas tank! The empty gas tank! What else?"

"I don't follow." He leaned toward her and she stared at him, speechless. "Well," he asked, "what about it? Did you talk to your teenage helper the

126

next day? What's his name, Bobby. I was called away in such a hurry that I didn't have time to find out if he messed up."

No you didn't, she thought. Just left a note. That way you didn't have to face me. How could he be so blatantly, immorally cool about having seduced her under false pretenses? And how he must have laughed at her on his way back to the city. Love-hungry widow...that must be how he saw her. Frustrated, probably. Did her a favor, did he? The memory burned.

"I don't want to be here with you," she said through clenched teeth. "And you know it."

"On the contrary. I don't know it. And I don't know why I should. I have no idea why you're upset with me, or why I deserve this cold shoulder treatment." He motioned to a hovering waiter and gave an order for two Black Russians. "You certainly didn't act this way on Sisters Island."

"No, unfortunately. But I should have, shouldn't I?" He looked so confused she was taken aback. "You're joking, surely."

He leaned forward and put his hand over hers on the table. "Courtney James, I honestly don't know what you're talking about."

She jerked her fingers from under his as though they burned. "Come on! You pretended we were out of gas to keep me on that island, and we both know it."

He shook his head, his jaw set. "I wouldn't have done such a ridiculous thing. You must know that."

He leaned forward and captured her hand again in both of his. Even though she tried to pull it away, a tingling rippled all through her arm when he touched her. Disgusted with herself, she shook her head. What was there about this man that turned her brain to mush? It wasn't going to happen again.

"Excuse me." She rose. "I'm leaving. Thanks for

your chivalrous offer, but I can find my own way to the Hyatt."

"Oh, no, you won't," he said, rising with her. "Not in Chicago at night, you won't. Your date left you in my care, and I don't take assignments like that lightly."

"My, my. Sir Galahad himself. Maybe you can have the cab run out of gas this time."

"Please, Courtney. What are you talking about?"

"You don't need to act the innocent. Bobby filled that tank before we took Andy water skiing. It couldn't have been out of gas. And let go of my hand. I'm leaving. If your Miss Georgie Burns can find her way around in Chicago alone, so can I."

"She's not my Georgie Burns. And besides, she's different."

"She certainly is."

"Courtney, listen. There was no gas. And that's that. Truth. Boy Scouts' honor." He held up three fingers. "Now, are you going to sit down and behave like a lady, or do you intend to flounce out of here like Georgie did? I hardly fancy causing two of the same sort of rows in one place. And, I must say, that kind of exit doesn't seem to fit your personality very well."

Embarrassed, Courtney glanced around at the curious faces turned toward them, obviously following this new discussion with undisguised interest between a second furious girl and the same calm escort. She sank grudgingly back in her chair.

He stood over her just long enough to make sure she stayed there before he sat down himself, waited a moment while a waiter set their drinks down, and then said, "And as for the gas tank, Miss James, if you'll take the trouble to check the slip in your till, I'm absolutely sure you'll find that to fill the tank in the morning took the whole ten gallons it can hold."

"Oh."

"Yes, oh."

"But—where did it go, then?" A tremendous relief swept through her. He hadn't lied. She hadn't realized until this moment how much she'd wanted that to be the case.

"I can't answer that right now, though when I think about it I have a pretty good idea. I believe I can find out. But not tonight, and not here." This time when he reached for her hand she didn't pull away. His eyes were devouring her whole being again and she had a difficult time pulling her gaze away from his. "Am I forgiven?"

She remembered his asking that on the first day they'd met. Sometimes it seemed that every one of his words was impressed in her memory. Feeling foolish, she gathered up her purse and wrap. "I'm ready to go back to my hotel. If you insist on escorting me, let's go now."

"Not just yet." He beckoned to the waiter to bring the check for the drinks. "I have a proposal to make."

"I'll bet."

"Tsk, tsk, Miss Suspicious. I heard you tell Andrews you wanted to see the town. Have you never?"

"No. I've been here, but only during the day." Glad to be on neutral ground, Courtney relaxed. "I suppose you have, many times."

He nodded, slid her drink across the table. "I live here and I've been around a bit. Enough to be able to show you a night you won't forget when you get back to Sister Bay. Come on, Courtney, how about it?" His grey eyes seemed bottomless. "Forget where we've been and where we're going and live for tonight." There was a husky magic in his voice, a magic she felt with every fiber of her being.

A night you won't forget. He'd said that about the sunset, and look where that had led. To a crazy sensuous, sexual encounter that had her whole equilibrium upset ever since.

"That's an irresponsible thing to do," she said, but a before-dinner cocktail, dinner champagne and a Black Russian was effectively lowering her defenses. She might not have another chance for a night she wouldn't forget...and it did sound attractive. She had so looked forward to this evening in Chicago.

"What do you suggest?" she asked.

"Whatever your fondest wishes might desire."

"Really." Courtney leaned back, observing how perfectly comfortable Lincoln Spencer looked in his tux. "Well. It's a warm July night. I'm in an exciting city. I'm blessed with a gentleman escort who won't take me home, and I'm promised an evening I won't forget. Quite a combination."

"Unbeatable."

She hesitated, studying the rugged planes of his face, the determined set of his jaw, the penetrating grey eyes, remembering the strength of his lean body. Forget where they'd been? Impossible. Live for tonight? Her resolve wavered, and, clinking her glass to his, she gave up, smiled tentatively and said, "Oh, why not? Onward, partner. Let's see your town."

His delight was evident, though she read it as victory. "You're on! And, first on the agenda, since my date for the evening skipped, as did yours." He pulled something from an inner pocket. "I just happen to have two tickets to the Schubert. It's a perennial favorite, 'Phantom of the Opera.' Have you seen it?"

"No. But I've always wanted to. I haven't seen any theater since I moved to the County. Oh, let's!" Courtney's eyes brightened with anticipation.

"A great beginning. I've been looking forward to the play, though I must admit that the prospect of seeing it with you instead of Georgie makes it sound a whole lot more enjoyable. Shall we?" He rose, bowed slightly, and crooked his arm.

Smiling, Courtney fitted her hand into the hollow of his elbow, feeling again that unexpected, electric warmth that seemed to charge from his body into hers. Heads turned as the striking couple, his dark head bent over her light one, moved toward the door.

Even if they had seen him, neither one would have taken note of the bald, gold-toothed man dining in a far corner. He scrubbed his ear with the flat of his palm as, with narrowed eyes, watched them leave.

Chapter Seventeen

"Wasn't Phantom grand, Link?" Courtney enthused as they flowed with the murmuring after-theater crowd onto Monroe Street where yellow cabs lined up for a half block waiting for fares. "What voices! What music! Thanks so much. I certainly didn't expect such a treat."

He took her arm, his smile as warm as the summer night air. "I'm glad you enjoyed it. It did make a nice beginning."

"Beginning! It's ten forty-five!"

"So?"

"So I'm usually either in bed already or well on my way."

"Maybe in Sister Bay this is the end of the evening. But here in Chicago, my little Chickadee—" He waggled his heavy brows in a poor imitation of WC Fields, "it's only a start."

"Oh? What if I'm tired?" teased Courtney. "I need my beauty sleep, you know?" But she was anything but sleepy. She was wound tight as a clock spring. The nearness of his handsomely clothed, lithe body was heady, though his friendly attitude—so far, at least—seemed to ask no more of her than enjoyment for an evening.

"Beauty sleep is one thing you don't need." He steered her around a clump of theater-goers. "Besides," he grinned, "we have a lot more to do before this evening is over."

She felt carefree and footloose, and full of the breathless excitement only this man seemed to bring out in her. But he's the one Lisbet has dibs on, Courtney reminded herself. She wasn't sure whether or not Link was aware of Lisbet's intentions, or whether he was susceptible to them or even wanted to be, but surely he was cognizant of her open admiration, and of her appreciation for his hours spent in teaching Andy to fish and row the skiff.

"He'll make a great father, won't he, Court?" Lisbet had asked one afternoon as they watched the two circle the dock in the small boat, Link patiently giving instructions and laughing with Andy as the little craft spun around in circles.

What had she answered? Courtney couldn't remember, but she could easily recall the wrench that had gone through her at Lisbet's remark.

"A penny for your thoughts?" Link questioned as he pulled her away from the bustling crowd. "Or are they worth more?"

"Probably not worth more," she answered, "but they're not for sale. It's such a lovely night, let's walk a little."

"I was hoping you'd want to. Michigan Avenue is this way. If we get tired we'll pick up a cab. We're going to have an after-show drink before the next lap of this marathon evening."

The streets were crowded with others like themselves, wandering through the balmy evening. Courtney was amazed at the number of people on the street. "I thought it would only be busy during working hours," she said, nearly tripping over a crack in the walk as she gawked up at the myriad lights above them. "Does it ever slow down?"

"Not for a while yet. I told you, it's early."

"Is your office near?" she asked as they wove through other pedestrians.

"Funny you should ask." They had reached a corner and were waiting for the light to change. He pointed. "Look up there. See the Prudential

Building? I'm on the thirty-second floor."

She squinted up at the well-lit building. "I'm impressed. Are you at the top?"

"Not quite, but close. The view of the lake used to be spectacular, but a lot of buildings have gone up and it's not as open as it was. Would you like to go up?"

"No, thanks." She had no intention of getting into an empty office building with him. A night on the town with plenty of people around was one thing; that might be quite another.

They had a brandy at a small, quiet lounge, enjoying its elegance and that of the well-dressed crowd around them, the understated music wafting through the shrubs and trees of an indoor garden. They talked about what Courtney had seen at the Sports show, how her ordered goods would fit into the next winter and summer seasons at Sister Bay. To her relief, he agreed with her choices. She'd been apprehensive of his disapproval at the amount she was investing, not that he had the right. But tonight, at least, he seemed content to leave the store operation to her discretion.

"And what brought you back to Chicago in such a hurry?" she asked.

"I was kidnapped."

She almost choked on her brandy. "Sure."

"Truth. Two people in a big car came to the cottage, said 'get in,' and I got in."

"Just like the Mafia in the movies. Be serious."

"I am. But that's not important now." Though he said it lightly, it was the truth. Georgie and her father had appeared on his doorstep, dressed for the city, only a few moments after Courtney had gone down to the store after their return from the island.

The judge had wheezed badly from the small effort of walking the short distance from his car to the cottage. "Get dressed and come along, Lincoln."

"Come where?"

"With me. Us. To the city."

"Why?"

"There are some men I want you to meet. Party men." The judge never wasted words; it was too laborious for him to speak at all.

"Hurry up, Linky! It's getting hot already," Georgie had complained.

"Just like that?" He had stared at the older man.

"Just like that. If you really want what you say you do." The judge turned slowly and walked toward his car. His labored breathing echoed in the quiet early morning air.

Lincoln had stared after him. Was this what it meant to be backed by power? To be ordered about like a lackey? He didn't like the feeling. Not at all.

Georgie waited for him as he dressed, her voice penetrating through his bedroom door. "Where were you last night, Linky?" she pouted. "I waited and waited, and then I came down here and you were gone."

"I had to meet a client," he lied. "And I was unexpectedly delayed." That part was true, at least. And thinking about it, he was pretty sure just who had caused that delay. Georgie had been standing by the ski boat when he left to dress to take Andy on the water. It would be like her to have drained the gas to make Courtney look less than efficient, just because she was another woman and someone he had contact with. Link grinned wryly to himself. If he was right, Georgie's scheme had certainly backfired, though he would probably never get her to admit to it.

"A client? Up here? So late?" Georgie had looked doubtfully at the wet swimsuit he tossed out onto the linoleum. "Were you swimming already this morning?" She sighed. "You sure are different when you're up here, Linky. I'll be glad to get you home where you belong." Where he belonged? More and more he was beginning to wonder just where that was.

Now he smiled at the lovely girl across the table from him tonight and changed the subject to a more pleasant one.

"Up and at 'em, Courtney James. There's a little after-theater eatery I mean to show you. Ready?"

Over her, "But I'm not hungry!" protests, Link ordered a late snack in the small, smoky side street cantina that specialized in authentic Mexican cuisine. "Just enough to give you strength to last the evening," he said as she warily eyed the steaming burrito smothered in cheese that was put in front of her. "We've hardly begun." To her surprise, she ate every bite.

They took a cab to the lakefront and wandered slowly and companionably along the park between bright city lights and dark water. The soft summer night enveloped them as they looked out over the lake, and it seemed to Courtney that time had no meaning until she barely stifled a yawn.

"I really have enjoyed this, but I think it must be time to call it a day—or a night. I've an early bus to catch. It must be well after midnight."

"Probably," said Link. "But I began ignoring my watch hours ago, and you're not wearing one, so how can we tell? There's lots of time left for a nightcap. And I know just the place."

The place was another small but uncrowded, softly-lit lounge where a guitar, piano and flute wove a quiet web of rhythm around them.

"What a nice choice," Courtney declared as they settled themselves at a tiny round table in a dim corner. "They're even playing my kind of music!" The musicians picked their way into the opening bars of *People*.

Link held out his hand, his grey gaze holding

her as he pulled her to her feet. "Dance." It wasn't a question.

Courtney looked up at him through a haze of new experiences and the drugging excitement of the city night and moved into his arms as though she belonged there. As his strong hand gently brought her head to rest on his shoulder, the flutist put aside her instrument and in a husky alto began to sing a well-known romantic song. Courtney closed her eyes and moved in Link's arms, the slow, rhythmic lyrics feeding into her drowsy wellbeing.

She thought fleetingly of Lisbet, back in Door County...and of Jerry Mitchell...of Logan Andrews, who had so willingly turned her over to Link this evening. Had that really been only a few hours ago?

Link murmured the song's tender words softly into her ear. The now-familiar warmth flushed through her body and Courtney nodded, her head moving slowly against his broad shoulder.

Laughing, he looked down. "Does that mean you're agreeing with the lyrics, or that you're about to fall asleep in my arms?"

Dreamily, Courtney upturned half-open dark-lashed aqua eyes. "Floating," she whispered. "Just floating."

His arms tightened around her, and Courtney stiffened. "I-I believe I'd better get back to my hotel."

"Not yet. Relax. The music hasn't ended." He brought her close again and Courtney moved with him, aware of the strength in his lean body and the easy elegance of his movements, enjoying the feelings that being in his arms brought to her body, yet thinking—knowing—she had no right...

The final notes drifted into the now-empty lounge and the musicians began to put away their instruments. The bartender, wiping up the last table, nodded a good night as they left.

Outside, the streets were still not empty. "It

does slow down," Courtney observed, fascinated with the city night. "Some."

"One more sight, and one more view," said Link. "Then I'll tuck you in."

Courtney raised her brows. "Figuratively, of course."

"Of course. If that's the way you want it."

His eyes were sending messages that made her ask herself, did she? Did she really want this evening to end?

"Where are we going?" she asked, as they turned into the lobby of the Hancock Center. "To a rooftop restaurant? Not another snack, please! I'm absolutely stuffed!" Acquiescent and mellow, she leaned against his sturdy shoulder and yawned as they waited for the elevator.

"No. Not quite." His voice held a huskiness that hadn't been there before. "But there's a view I want you to see."

"From?" She let the question hang in the air as she watched the elevator indicator flicker up, up to 83 before it stopped.

"This way." Spencer led her down a short hall.

Almost too tired to care, Courtney leaned against the wall, watching him open the door. "What sort of place is this? It had better be good." She yawned again.

They entered a small apartment which opened into a tiny kitchenette, passed that door into a small but perfectly appointed living room furnished with a comfortable-looking beige velour couch and overstuffed chairs scattered with blue velvet pillows. Two lamps and a coffee table completed the furnishings, though Courtney scarcely noticed them because the whole far wall was glass.

She walked to the window as though in a dream. The scene was breathtaking. Below her the city reached as far as she could see in any direction, a blanket of millions of lights: red, green, amber, fabulous neons. Automobiles trailed red streaks as they threaded through darkened streets; office windows darkened one by one as cleaning crews finished their tasks.

"It—it's unbelievable!" Courtney breathed, her eyes wide, every sense awakened to the pulse of this magnificent city. She was wrapped in a rich cocoon high above Chicago, and the city was hers to savor. She reveled in the scene spread below her like a sparkling, moving quilt, conscious that Link was somewhere behind her but not really paying him any attention until his fingers curled hers around a long-stemmed glass of bubbling liquid.

"A toast. To Chicago," he said, "and a wonderful evening with a perfect companion." He touched the rim of his glass to hers, sending a small, clear chime through the room.

"Thank you." Courtney lifted the chilled champagne to her lips and her shining aqua eyes sparkled like the wine. "An evening always to be remembered as I nod off in front of the fire in my little log cottage in the woods."

"And one for me to remember from wherever I happen to be. My thanks to you, Courtney James. I'd forgotten, in the everyday rat race, and in dealing with a lot of ordinary and sometimes cantankerous people, what a charming city Chicago can be."

Courtney turned again to the window. "It's like fairyland, isn't it?" she whispered. For the first time she noticed soft music coming from a wall speaker. "Whose place is this?"

"Mine. I often have out of town clients who need a place to stay or hold a small, private meeting. Here is where I put them up."

"Lucky clients. I wonder if they are all as impressed as I." Courtney leaned her forehead against the window glass. "It's strange. I don't believe I've ever done as much, eaten as much, or had as many different drinks in one night as I have tonight, yet I've never felt better. There's something special in the air."

"It's the company," he broke in, smiling, "isn't it? But you are tired. Your glass is tipping." He gently removed it from her hand and set it on the window ledge next to his own. Then he took both her hands in his. "Courtney."

Her eyes rose to his. "No, Link..." But she couldn't move away. Her betraying body remembered and ached for his arms, his mouth, his touch, all of him that he was willing to give.

"Don't say anything. Not now." He reached behind her head to undo the silver barrette that held her hair. Gently, he threaded his fingers through the shiny golden mass and shook it loose until it fell in waves over her shoulders and down her back.

"So beautiful." He brought her to him, his lips first touching hers gently, a whispered promise, then moving up her face lightly, and finally kissing her eyes closed, murmuring, "Such an impossible color. I dream about your eyes."

Courtney began to float, reliving this evening and that other evening under the stars. Only this time we're over instead of under them, she thought. His mouth is wonderful...his arms are so strong...the city is ours...a night to enjoy.

His moist lips brushed her earlobe, moved down her slender throat. "You must know I've thought of nothing but you since the island. I had to leave, but I didn't want to." He held her wrists behind her back as he pressed his lean, hard body to hers. She felt his arousal and her desire rose to meet it. "You do want me," he whispered. "You do."

Even if she had wanted to say no, had wanted to remember her promise to Lisbet, there was no way her heated body would listen. Courtney's mind swirled, but she knew it wasn't from the evening's drinks. Her breasts arched toward him, and he bent to nuzzle their tips into hard nubbles of desire through the thin turquoise of her evening dress.

"Come." He led her into a darkened room which seemed to be all bed except for a small space near the large window where he stood behind her, his arms caressing the rounded mounds of her desirous breasts as she faced the brilliant city lights. The only illumination came from below, an ever-changing intensity that only added to the electricity in the room high above.

"My golden goddess," he murmured, kissing the top of her head. "Don't move. Let your mind float among those lights below as it floated in the Northern Lights."

His voice was low and dreamlike. She nodded, remembering. She felt his fingers slowly, teasingly slip her straps from her shoulders. His sensuous fingertips followed down her back as he unzipped her dress, as his palms slid around her waist and moved up ever so slowly to cup her breasts and to tease their hardened nipples softly between his thumbs and forefingers.

A small sigh escaped her lips as he laid a finger across her mouth. "Shhh." His voice was so husky with desire that she shivered from head to foot. An ache whirled through her and settled in the very center of her being, and she tried to turn into his arms.

"No, no," he whispered. "Don't move. Don't talk. Let me tease you. I want you beyond speaking, and I'll make you want me that much, too."

But I do, she thought, a shiver of anticipation shuddering through her, I do. Changing lights from the city below shimmered on the white band of her untanned breasts as his fingers slipped into the waistband of her half-slip and pantyhose. His palms smoothed them off her hips as his moist moving lips followed them down lightly, touching the quivering muscles of her back and down her thighs. Her body pushed toward his palms, aching for more.

"Oh," she moaned, her head back, eyes closed. "It's not fair. I can't reach you."

"Shhh. You will." His forefinger pressed her lips for a moment before he moved around her and knelt, gently lifting one foot to slip her stocking off, then the other. He stood back, his eyes roving over her beauty. "My lovely goddess...reach me now. Move now for me."

"Yes."

She stretched her arms above her head, arching her back, feeling bathed in beauty, then, opening her arms, stepped toward him, lifting her face to invite his descending mouth.

City light flickered over and around them. Sister Bay and Lisbet were part of another world, another life, in this moment out of time. "If I am a goddess, then you are a god," she whispered, her lips bruised, swollen with desire as she slipped his jacket from his shoulders. "Slowly, Lincoln..."

"Slowly. Stay with me, Courtney."

"Yes."

She raised herself on tiptoes against him, loving the feeling of her body against his, climbing his desire as she ascended her own in this fairyland far above the stars of Chicago.

Chapter Eighteen

The bell that roused Courtney from sleep wasn't a familiar one. She moved her cheek, nuzzling into what she thought was her pillow, but something tickled her nose and she opened her eyes to realize her head was resting on Lincoln Spencer's darkly furred chest and the sweet smell of lovemaking was thick around them.

The bell rang again. "Link! Link, wake up!" She shook him awake. "The phone!"

"Ummmm." He pulled her close and kissed the top of her tousled head as he reached for the bedside instrument, holding her closely in the crook of his arm while he answered, his voice still rough with sleep. "Hello?....No, but I can probably find out...What? Andy! When?" His eyes, wide awake now, met Courtney's startled ones, but he motioned her to silence and held her even tighter against his chest. "I'll find her, Lisbet, don't worry about that, and we'll be there as soon as we can. Hold on...don't lose your grip. Is anyone there with you?...Jerry? Oh, yes, Mitchell. Good. Have you contacted authorities? Both Police and Coast Guard? Good...Yes. Hold tight, okay? We'll be there soon...No, we'll fly. Have Mitchell meet us at the Gibraltar Airport in two hours...don't apologize, for God's sake, Lisbet! I love that kid, too. We're on our way."

He put the phone back on its cradle and, flinging the rumpled quilt aside, got up and strode to the dresser for his watch. "Almost noon!"

The sight of his elegant nude body sent a shiver

143

through Courtney even as she asked, "What is it?" Eyes wide, hair disheveled, her face appealingly flushed from sleep, Courtney propped herself on one elbow, holding the covers high across her naked breasts. In the light of morning her being here in Lincoln Spencer's bed didn't seem right. "What about Andy? Is he hurt?"

"I don't know. I hope not. He's gone." Link pulled open a drawer and dug out a pair of jeans and a flannel shirt.

"Gone! What do you mean?"

"That's all I know. He wasn't there when Lisbet woke up this morning. She's frantic, as you can imagine, trying to get hold of you, and when you weren't at your hotel, she called my answering service, hoping I could find you." His voice was muffled as he pulled on his shirt. "She thinks he may have gone out in one of the fishing skiffs because the little one he plays around in was found washed up on shore a half-mile down toward town."

"Oh, Link! No! Not Andy!"

Less than an hour later she was checked out of her hotel, had called Lisbet to assure her they were coming and carefully sidestepped an answer to how Lincoln had found her so quickly. He had arranged to have his Piper Cherokee ready to fly the minute they hit the airport.

A fierce wind buffeted the small plane as they swung out in an arc toward Lake Michigan, pulled back over the city and headed north. Courtney shuddered involuntarily as she looked into the western sky where an ominous pile of boiling black clouds rolled toward them at an alarming rate.

She pictured little Andy, trying to imagine where he might have gone. Please God, she prayed that he wasn't in that boat. Surely he wouldn't have tried to go out without a life jacket. That was a rule he positively knew she never let anyone disobey, no matter how good a swimmer they claimed to be. But the jackets were kept in the locked store at night.

"Bad weather on the way," Link said through a tight jaw. "If we'd have waited to leave a half hour later we'd have been grounded. Lisbet said they had a terrific storm up on the peninsula last night and another is blowing in. This—" he indicated the clouds swirling toward them, "is probably part of it. I hope we can beat it."

"Oh! Then maybe the boat just blew out. Perhaps Liss hadn't secured it well. Do you know if Andy was home then? During the storm?"

"I don't know. It's certainly possible that the skiff washed out by itself and has nothing to do with Andy."

"I hope so—OH!" Courtney gasped and grabbed for the hand grip above her window as they dropped into an air pocket that left her stomach hanging somewhere above her for seconds before it resumed its proper place.

"Sorry," he said, grimacing. "Those drops always come as a surprise. Okay?"

She nodded, swallowing. "I am now. Don't mind me. I've never flown in a small plane before," she said as the first burst of rain hit the windshield like a deluge, "let alone in a hurricane. Oh, I'm so glad Jerry is there with Liss. You know how she is about Andy even when he's fine. And Jerry is wonderful in a crisis."

"Really?" He gave her a probing look. "How do you know?"

She hesitated, reluctant to reopen the door on unhappy memories. "It's a long story and I won't bore you with all of it. When Ronnie was killed, Jerry was there every minute when I needed him. I loved him for it." Her mind pictured Jerry at the hospital, at the funeral home, as the hot summer wind had ruffled his fair hair the day they scattered

Ronnie's ashes. Back in time for the moment, Courtney stared unseeingly out at the grey swirls enveloping the plane and was startled when Link's rough voice interrupted her thoughts.

"And do you love him now?"

"What?" Surprised, she turned to Link but he was checking gauges and didn't meet her eyes. "I don't think you have the right to ask that."

"Sorry. Overstepped my bounds, did I?"

She looked down toward the ground but there was nothing to see but grey smoky swirling clouds. "Not really. I'd just like to think you would understand this past week couldn't have happened if I loved someone. Jerry's my friend, my buddy. That's all." She picked at a speck of lint on her slacks, tears filling her eyes. Little Andy declared he was her buddy, too. "Oh, Link, Andy's such a good little boy!"

"I know." He reached over to cover her hand with his. "God willing, we'll find him and he'll be fine. He's probably just exploring somewhere. It's only been a few hours. A little guy like that can get interested in watching something and lose all track of time." He put his warm hand over hers. "Why don't you rest? You didn't get much sleep last night."

Guilt spread through Courtney like a flame, reliving the passionate hours in his suite above the flickering city. The knowledge of her deception to Lisbet would hurt at the best of times, and now, with Andy in trouble, perhaps hurt, perhaps even...dead. "Don't," she said shortly, pulling her hand away.

"Don't?" He raised his brows.

"It was just another starry night, another romantic interlude. A fantastic evening on the town that I enjoyed very much. It didn't mean a thing."

"It was more than that," he said quietly. "Both times." Her face was turned away from him, but she knew he caught her gesture as she wiped away the tear that threatened to escape down her cheek. "And you know it."

"But Lisbet—" she blurted, then bit her lip.

"We'll help her find Andy, of course. But that has nothing to do with us." The line of his jaw was hard.

Oh, yes, it does, thought Courtney. You just don't understand. She leaned back against the seat, her eyes closed, her mind a jumble of memories, thinking over all the years that had molded her protective feelings for little Lisbet, who had never quite gotten what she wanted, who had always made the wrong choices and then had to pay for them. All through life, Lisbet had had a rotten time. Now she was free to make a good life for herself and she deserved it.

I've spent most of my life doing my best to give her anything I could, thought Courtney. I can't just stop now. I've taught her to expect it.

Courtney opened her eyes to look at Link's scowling face and told herself, he's Lisbet's, she wants this man and I've denied all interest. She needs him, and Andy needs the kind of father he will be. Didn't I hear him tell her he loved Andy, too? And Lisbet trusts me. Me! Who's been held in Lincoln Spencer's arms and loved every second of it; who's thrown care away and given him freely everything I have.

A sudden squall hit the plane and its wings dipped crazily before Link righted it and regained control. "You deny we're good together?" he asked, raising his voice over the sound of the plane and the buffeting winds.

She gripped the edge of her seat. "So? There's more to living than sex."

"Sex? Is that what we had? I thought there was a good deal more to it than that."

If I only hadn't promised Lisbet, she thought...but that was before I knew—a sudden burst of rain sheeted across the windshield at the same time realization burst on Courtney and she turned quickly to his dark profile—knew that I would love you!

She caught her breath. Had she spoken aloud? No. He was studying the controls, his jaw set in a grim line.

"Love 'em and leave 'em, is that it?" His grey eyes, darker than the stormy sky, probed hers. "Sex for fun and games? Somehow that doesn't seem your style."

"My style! You've been trying to tell me what my style is ever since I met you! What if I just want a good time once in a while, no strings attached?"

"Is that what you want?"

No, no, she told herself. I want you, your home, your sturdy children. I want you to be the father of my son, not someone else's. Aloud, she said firmly, "I won't see you alone again."

"And that's that." He wrestled with the controls as another sweep of wind buffeted the plane. "So easy for you, isn't it?"

No! If he only knew how hard it was to say the words, make them sound sincere. "Yes. That's that."

"Would you care to tell me why?"

Why? Tell him why? She fidgeted with her purse. Because I love you, and because I made a promise to my little sister. Because I'm the strong one, I can make it alone. Because she needs you. Andy needs you.

Link reached over and turned her tear-streaked face to his, but she kept her eyes closed. It would hurt too much to look into those grey, bottomless ones that could read her mind.

"No answer?" He flicked his hand away from her as though to remove any trace of her from his fingers and turned his head away. "We'll leave it at that, then. If that's the way you want it." He turned his complete attention to flying the plane through the storm.

Judge Adam Burns set aside the Sunday morning paper and looked up appreciatively as his daughter—wearing an ostrich-feathered royal blue satin dressing gown that accentuated her ripe curves—drooped into the dining room in their Lake Forest home. She would have been elegantly beautiful except for the dark rings that circled her blue eyes.

He cleared his phlegmy throat, gurgling a greeting. "'Morning, Honey."

"Not much of a good one, Daddy. I hate this dreary rain." Georgie plopped down on an antique chair and motioned the white-aproned maid to fill her coffee cup. "Just a muffin, Sarah."

"Just a muffin? Dieting?" he smiled. "You don't need to."

"I'm not hungry."

"Rough night?"

No answer. Judge Burns studied his only daughter. God, she was the picture of her mother. Not as tall, but so much the same. Not as soft, though, not as sweet. Laura. He sighed, almost saying her name aloud. How he wished she were still with him. She'd know what to do with a daughter like Georgie. Most of the time he was at a loss. "I had a call from Hank McGee this morning." He stopped to pull enough air into his lungs to continue. Damn it, each day now it seemed his condition worsened.

"So? Who's he?" Georgie disinterestedly buttered her muffin and picked off a small bit to put in her mouth.

"Just a friend. Business associate."

"And?" She raised her eyebrows and stirred a heaping spoonful of sugar into her coffee.

Judge Burns hesitated. He didn't like meddling in other people's lives, but by God he was going to see his daughter settled before he breathed his last hard breath. "He had dinner at the Palmer Hotel last night."

Georgie's eyes widened, met his for a guilty moment, then looked away. "Really?"

"Really." The Judge leaned forward, putting his beefy hand over her red-tipped one. "It seems you made quite a little scene with our Lincoln."

"Oh!" Georgie threw her napkin down on the tabletop and stomped toward the French doors at one end of the room. She stood, her back ramrod stiff, staring out at the small formal garden. "Our Lincoln! Well, I guess there's more truth than fiction in that." She turned to face her father. "Tell me, whose is he, Daddy? Mine? Or yours?"

"What do you mean?"

"You know what I mean. I want him, but you've got him. Right by his elegant balls."

"Georgie!"

"Sorry."

"Come on, Honey. Tell me about last night."

She slumped back down on the chair. "What's to tell? I'm crazy about the man, you know that. But he's not crazy about me. He only humors me because of you." She put her elbows on the table and dropped her chin onto her palms. "Oh, Daddy, I want him so much and he's so...so unreachable! Even more since he's been spending time up in that awful little Sister Bay! He's just so...so—impossible!"

Judge Burns leaned back, his eyes narrowing. "In what way?"

"You said he was going to marry me. That he wanted to. Well, he's had every opportunity to ask. I've practically asked him. Nothing. And now—you should have heard him last night!—now he keeps talking about how great that little hick town up north is, and wouldn't it be fun to live there. There of all places!"

"Live there?" The judge gargled a cough and took a swallow of coffee to clear his throat. "In Sister Bay?"

"Sure. Can't you just see me there! Maybe I could learn to make quilts, or—or weave baskets. Paint lousy pictures of the tourists going by."

"But his career is here. I've got it all worked out, everything! The political backing, even the money for getting into the race next year. Christ! I've even set him up in our corporation. I've done everything I can to push him!"

"Maybe he's not impressed. It's me, Daddy. I thought I could make him love me, and I can't....Oh, I don't know!"

The judge sighed. "Hank told me something else I think you should hear."

Georgie looked up. "What?"

"It seems that after you stormed out, our Lincoln joined the girl from the Sister Bay fishing goods place. You know the one. What she was doing here, I don't know." The judge paused. "Her escort left. And then...they left together. She and Lincoln."

Georgie stared at her father for a second, then burst into tears and ran from the room. The old man stared after her for a moment, then, rising with difficulty, called after her, "Don't you worry about Lincoln, Georgie. I'll see about him." Gasping, he sank back on his chair. "And I will see," he said softly, "about her, too.

Chapter Nineteen

Jerry Mitchell was parked at the end of the runway in Lisbet's Volkswagen when Link's Piper Cherokee dropped unsteadily down through turbulent low clouds and coasted to a stop only feet from the end of the small grass-spiked asphalt strip. It was obvious from Jerry's worried expression as he ran toward the plane that Andy was still missing.

"They haven't found him!" Courtney covered her face with her hands. "Oh, Link!"

Link cut the motor to an idle. As Jerry hurried to the plane and wrenched open the door to help Courtney out, the wind gusted a chilling burst of rain over them in the cockpit.

Unbuckling her safety belt, Courtney turned to Link, who hadn't yet unfastened his. "Link—" She wanted to say something, but, given their last conversation, was at a loss. There had been nothing but chill in the plane since he had agreed to her terms, and the last half hour had seemed endless. Her eyes pleaded his understanding but only met his cool grey gaze.

"Out. Mitchell's waiting for you."

She stared at him. "For you, too. Aren't you coming?"

"Hurry up, Court!" Jerry yelled over the wind and rain, reaching into the plane for her hand. "I'm getting soaked!"

"Aren't you coming?" she repeated. Was Lincoln that furious with her that he would abandon the search for Andy?

"No. I'm going up again."

"Up! In this!" It was even more windy here, gusting off the bay with terrific force, and the rain stabbed at them in solid sheets. "Why?"

"Think, Courtney. You remember last week, when Andy said he bet he was strong enough now to row all the way to those little outcroppings down toward Horseshoe Island? He wanted to explore like Huckleberry Finn. I'm thinking he might just have done that. If he did try to take the boat there early this morning and the wind picked up like this, he might have been stranded. If he's there, there's not much cover. I'll be able to see him from the air."

"But it's so wild, Link. And it's getting so dark already. The wind's worse every minute! You'll be blown into the bluffs!" Courtney's eyes were dark with worry.

She does care, he thought. At least a little. There wasn't time now to get to the bottom of her refusal to see him again, but he would deal with her later, after they found Andy.

"Think of the boy, Court. What if he's out there, in this storm? He'll be terrified." A flash of lightning and its nearly simultaneous thunder punctuated his words. "I can't set down to pick him up, but he'll know someone found him, and that should help. He'll know we'll be back. Now get going. Lisbet needs you."

Courtney heard concern for Lisbet underlying his words. Of course. For a moment she had forgotten of whose future he was meant to be part.

"Sorry," she said stiffly, and climbed out of the cockpit to run through the blustering squall with Jerry. As he turned the little car around to drive toward Sister Bay she craned her neck to watch as the light Cherokee struggled to pull up into the storm. Its wings tipped dangerously at the end of the runway as the wind buffeted it from one side, and for a moment she thought it would be forced into the trees at the edge of the airfield. As she held her breath, the plane pulled away just in time and rose over the trees with only a few feet to spare. Courtney didn't realize how hard she had been biting her lip until she tasted her own blood.

Tree limbs along the highway whipped wildly, and Jerry struggled to keep the lightweight little car from being blown off the road as they sped toward Sister Bay.

"Thank God you've come, Court. Lisbet's going crazy." His eyes narrowed for better vision through the rain. "I wanted her to come with me but she was determined to stay by the telephone in the store."

"The police? And the Coast Guard?"

"Both searching. She wanted to be there if there was any word." Jerry stared grimly through the nearly obliterated windshield. His voice was rough with emotion. "She's been a brick, as much as she can be, but you know how she is about Andy. And I am, too, I guess," he confessed. "If anything's happened to that sweet little kid..."

"We just have to believe it hasn't," Courtney declared, though it seemed impossible that Andy could be all right if he was out in this dangerous weather. He was healthier and stronger now, but he'd been so sick, and so fragile...if he got wet and cold the asthma could turn into pneumonia.

She turned wide eyes to Jerry and put a hand on his arm. "Oh, Jerry, do you think Link will be all right?"

Jerry pulled his attention from what he could see of the road and cocked an eyebrow at her. "So it's 'Link' now, is it?" He turned back to his mission again, but not before he asked, "You care a lot about that guy, don't you?"

Did it show? "I'd care about anybody who took a little airplane up in this!"

"Sure, sure."

Was Jerry jealous? It really didn't sound like it. Maybe he wasn't going to keep on declaring his love for her; that would be a relief. "When did you come up, Jerry?"

"Friday, late. We've been having a good weekend—until today."

"We?"

"Lisbet and Andy and me." He took his attention off driving long enough to pat her arm in a brotherly way. "Listen. Spencer will be okay. I've heard he's a pro when it comes to flying."

"Pro or not, this is no weather to be proving it."

"Right about that. Whew!" A fallen birch branch rolled along like a tumbleweed ahead of the car on the steep hill road to the shore and Jerry slowed, leaving time for it to career off the road into the woods. He braked to a stop in the small parking lot of Courtney's Sports. "Thank God, here we are."

They waited for the thunder that came too soon after a blinding flash of lightning before they dashed into the store to find a drenched Lisbet sitting on the high stool behind the counter with her head in her hands. She raised a tear-stained face and ran around to counter into Courtney's arms. "Oh, Court!" she wailed. "What can we do?"

"No word? From either the police or the guard?"

"Nothing. I'm going insane! He's so little, and he's all alone, wherever he is, and you know how easily he gets that asthma, or a panic attack, and it's wet, and cold—" Lisbet's teeth were chattering, and her last bit of reserve crumpled as she sobbed into Courtney's shoulder.

"Take her up to her cottage, Jerry, and put her in a hot tub. I'll wait here," said Courtney. "It won't do to have two to take care of when we find Andy. Get hold of yourself, Liss, and go with Jerry. Now!"

Lisbet nodded and moved docilely in Jerry's

protective arm. As they went out the door, she turned, her eyes so full of anguish they brought sympathetic tears to Courtney's. "Thanks for coming back, Court. I knew I could count on you."

Her words stuck like sharp knives into her conscience. Count on her! After the island! After last night! Lisbet would have better luck counting on a rattlesnake.

Courtney sank down behind the checkout counter where Lisbet had been sitting. Over the wild wind and the crash of waves along the shore, she thought she heard the whine of a small airplane. She ran to the window but saw nothing except pounding rain and, try hard as she would, she didn't hear the sound again. Link could be down, in those wild, cold waves—or caught like a colorful butterfly in a net, somewhere in the top of the enormous white pines that lined the shore farther down. A wind like this could master any pilot, no matter how professional.

Courtney dropped her head into her palms. Andy, Andy, she prayed, be all right.

Suddenly, with the quickness of the bursting flashes of lightning that were coming closer and more frequently now, she thought of Andy's game. Where was he? If only this was just a game...if he were only just hiding. What if he really was exploring a hiding place, and something had happened? What if he had gotten into someplace where he couldn't get out—she'd heard about things like that, kids crawling into old refrigerators or freezers. But were there any of those around? She didn't think so.

A picture of Andy's little freckled face appeared in her mind, and she remembered the last time they'd played the game, when she had chided him for pretending to be in a cave up the hill. "No fair! It has to be a real place, Andy!" she'd said.

"But it is, Auntie Court! It really is!" His blue

eyes had seemed enormous in his suntanned face. "It's right behind that one big tree!"

Maybe it really was. Behind one big tree in the midst of so many.

Maybe he was there, someplace up the hill, caught in a cave. Perhaps hurt. Maybe right now he was sending her an ESP signal from wherever he was. She felt a pull toward the bluff that was almost as strong as the storm's winds, as though she heard his small voice calling to her.

Courtney stared out the window at the whitecaps pounding over the dock. Lightning skittered down the black, boiling sky and sizzled into the water on the far side of the bay; thunder followed almost instantly. The central force of the storm was closer by the minute. She couldn't remember another that had been this fierce for this long.

Courtney shut her eyes. There were at least a hundred big trees on the hillside bluff. If there was a cave...she could try to find it, but dare she leave the telephone? What if the someone called and no one were here? She would call them and check the status of the search.

It was now so dark in spite of the afternoon hour that Courtney had to snap on the overhead light to check the number. She picked up the instrument, listened for the tone and began to dial, but a too-close zigzag spear of lightning flashed; a simultaneous deafening clap of thunder rolled away and the phone in her hand went dead.

An omen. There was no need to stay with it now. She had to try to find Andy. And since there was no one to help, she would manage alone.

Courtney's driving-to-the-city slacks and blouse were hardly warm enough, but she slipped on her work sweatshirt and unbuckled her dress sandals, stubbing her nyloned feet into her sand-stained boating tennies. She grabbed her yellow slicker off the hook in the washroom, snapped it shut and tied a short piece of line around her waist to make it snug against the wind. She pulled the hood tight around her face and knotted it under her chin.

She started out the door, but at the last minute went back to the checkout counter to rip a sheet from a sales pad and scribble on the back, "Checking the bluff. Andy talked about a cave." She laid the note by the phone and snatched up a small flashlight, along with a slightly melted Hershey bar. If she did find Andy, they might help.

Courtney pulled the door closed behind her and gasped as the full force of the storm lashed her unprotected face. The temperature must have dropped twenty degrees. The enormous white pines on the hillside bluff danced dervishly as the wind and rain buffeted them from all sides. Lightning flickered and sizzled constantly, and she thought wryly that out here, at least, she certainly wasn't going to need the flashlight.

She raised her chin resolutely and, grasping underbrush alongside the narrow path to keep her balance against the gusts, started climbing toward the rough terrain behind the cottages. Surely Andy was sending her signals, or she wouldn't be so certain of where to look. A wet branch slapped her in the face and she slipped backwards for a moment before regaining her balance. She hardly noticed.

I'm coming, Andy, she mentally telegraphed ahead. If there is a cave, I'll find it.

Chapter Twenty

Though Courtney had climbed the hill to her cottage many times, she had never attempted to go above it. The incline steepened sharply, changing from a gentle rise with fairly sparse undergrowth to an almost perpendicular bluff of stone outcroppings with scrub underbrush thick between fallen timbers and the sturdy trunks of tall white pines. Footing was treacherous where downed wood had rotted away leaving deep, uneven hollows under a solid-looking surface.

There didn't seem to be enough topsoil to hold such large trees here. She toiled up the incline, stumbling into hidden crevices, which roots had once filled. The wind whipped into the bluff full force, tearing at the tops of the evergreens above her head, forcing a high whine from the branches that was painful compared to the soft, soughing whisper Courtney was used to hearing as a backdrop against Door County's usually quiet summer days and nights.

Gusts of rain pounded against the slick plastic of her headgear, making it difficult to ascertain whether there was any answer to her frequent calls.

"An—dy! An—dy!" She called over and over, but as soon as she opened her mouth her voice was torn away and swallowed by the deafening wind and thunder.

"He'll never hear me," she anguished aloud but that, too, was born away on a swoop of wind that splatted a bucketful of rain from the foliage of a low hazelnut bush into her face. She wiped her eyes with the backs of her hands and continued combing the incline in as straight a line across it as she could follow back and forth above both the cottages, certain that Andy wouldn't have gone much beyond the far limits of either one, though he might have climbed high behind them on the bluff itself.

Her tennis shoes were soaked, her feet freezing. She should have had enough sense to pull on some rubber boots. No matter. At least she was safe on the ground. Was Link? Surely we would have come back by now. If he made it back at all.

"An—dy! An—dy!" she called, then untied her hood and pushed it back to clear her ears while she waited for an answering shout. If he could hear her, and if he was all right enough to answer, she thought grimly.

Lightning cracked so close that it must have hit something nearby, perhaps directly above her on the bluff. Thunder was almost simultaneous again, and deafening. She cringed against the trunk of a tree and waited until the last of the sound rumbled away before calling again.

"An—dy! Can you hear me?" Her voice was becoming hoarse. The wind lessened for a few seconds, but though she strained to listen she heard no answer. Somewhere behind her a rending screech like splintering wood, then a crash told her a sizeable tree had blown down. She scanned those whipping above her, but they seemed strong enough to withstand the wind.

Panting now, moving foot by foot, tree by tree, sometimes circling ten feet out of her planned line because of heavy underbrush or washed gullies that were too difficult to maneuver, Courtney made her way slowly and painstakingly back and forth over the heavily wooded acreage, stopping every few feet, calling, pulling off her hood to listen, going on...calling...trudging on.

Her breath came harder now. The storm showed no sign of lessening. She stopped momentarily to lean against the trunk of an ancient tree. Her long hair, whipped to wet snarls, was impossible to push back into her hood; she gave up the idea and left it down. Shivering, she took deep breaths to steady herself and shrieked as a dead branch hurtled down through the pine above her and fell within a few feet of where she stood.

Better to keep moving. So tired...how long had she been out? Probably not even an hour, though it seemed like forever. Frustration and ineffectiveness flooded through her chilled body like a torrent, and she pounded her fists against the rough bark of an ancient white pine, stuck out her chin and yelled into the swirling rain and wind, "I won't stop until I've covered this hill! Do you hear me? I won't! Go ahead! Blow! I'm not afraid! I'm not!"

The wind abated momentarily, and she almost laughed at herself for being so foolish, shouting at the elements as though she could make them understand. But wait!

What was that? Courtney tilted her head, holding her long wet hair away from her ears. There it was again! Could it be...

"Andy! An—dy!" She shut her eyes tight, willing to better hear as the wind picked up again and tore her words away...but...yes! His small voice came at her from...where?

"Auntie Court! Auntie Court! I'm here!"

Relief took the stiffening out of her legs for a moment, and she blinked as a frightening flash of lightning with its accompanying thunder crack rolled over all her senses before she looked frantically in every direction. "Where are you, Champo?" Her voice was strained. "I can't find you! Keep calling, don't stop!"

"I will, I will! Here, Auntie Court, down here!

His voice was faint, and whirled by the wind until she had no idea from which direction it came. She turned full circle, scanning every inch of ground. "Where? Where shall I look? Tell me!"

She cupped her ears to catch his faint, wind-blown words. "There's a hole! Under a big old tangled-up root behind that one big tree! Remember, I told you! Oh, please help me, Auntie Court, I'm so cold!"

"I'm coming, Andy. I see the root!" Courtney scrambled over a fallen log to the overturned root of a great pine that had fallen, probably years ago. Its wood was a weather-bleached web at least a dozen feet across. A brilliant flash of lightning illuminated a small, deep opening in the bluff bedrock behind its cover, an opening so well hidden she would never have found it on her own. Kneeling on the wet pine-needled ground, she peered into the hole but could see nothing. "Andy? Are you here? Are you all right? Are you hurt?"

His voice sounded hollow, as if echoing off wet walls. "No, but I'm really really cold. Oh, Auntie Court, you found me. Come get me out!"

"I will, Champo. Hold on." Oblivious now to the rain and wind, Courtney reached into the hole as far as she could, but felt nothing but cool underground air. She dug in her pocket for the flashlight and shone it into the opening, which appeared to angle down for a couple of feet and then disappeared into a void.

"Coming, Andy." She got down on all fours and squeezed her shoulders into the opening, crawling in on the wet, mud-covered surface. Suddenly her hands shot out in front of her and the flashlight rolled away. Reaching to catch it, she fell onto the front of her slicker. Its smooth wet surface acted like a water slide. In seconds she had tumbled headfirst over the edge and somersaulted into a deep, dark hole.

Her ankle hurt like fury, and she gasped with pain as she looked up into the light that Andy was now holding next to his dirty, tear-stained face. He leaped into her arms, shivering. He was dressed only in shorts and a light tee shirt. "Oh, thank you, Auntie Court. I thought and thought, you know, about you thinking I was hiding..." His arms were around her neck in a strangling bear hug. He stopped to take a breath and she winced as she heard the too-familiar wheezing rasp that came so often when he was overtired or worried. "...and I knew you would come!"

She had come, all right, a lot farther than she intended. Courtney rubbed her ankle. It didn't feel broken, but she certainly had given it a twist. At least Andy wasn't hurt. She put as much bravado into her voice as she could, given the circumstances. "Hand me that light, Andy, and let's see where we are."

She hugged the small, shivering boy close to her as she shone the inadequate light beam around the bowl-shaped hole that imprisoned them. It appeared to be about eight feet across, and at least a dozen feet deep, with no outlet except the one she had so inadvertently come down. Even if she could put Andy on her shoulders, he wouldn't be able to reach the lip. And if he could, the mud was probably too slippery for him to crawl out.

"Lucky neither one of us was badly hurt by falling down here," she said, attempting to put a smile in her voice. "Well. Now it looks as though we're both holed up where nobody can find us, doesn't it? A fine rescuer I am, huh, Andrew Grant?" She gave his thin shoulders a reassuring hug, but didn't feel very reassured herself. If they could outlast this storm, perhaps when it was quiet outside again they could set up a howling duet that would surely bring someone. She listened, but heard no evidence of the storm's abating; thunder roiled almost constantly, shaking even their underground shelter, and if anything, the lightning flashes that were steadily illuminating even their prison seemed to be closer than before. Lisbet had said they'd been told this storm was to be the worst the peninsula had ever suffered, and it certainly seemed that it was just that.

The boy took a labored breath and his voice shook as he asked, "Won't they find us, Auntie Court? You did. Where's my mom? Is Mr. Jerry still with her? He won't let anything happen to us, will he?"

"Not if he can help it, I'm sure. Come here, you must be freezing." She opened her coat and Andy huddled inside her large sweater with her, his small body convulsively shaking with chills. They would have to get out of here soon or he would contract pneumonia as he had earlier in the year.

"Let's turn off that light. We may need it later," she said.

"It's awful dark without it," Andy whispered.

And damp, she added to herself. And cold and miserable and her ankle was throbbing like crazy and nobody in the world knew where they might be. Aloud she put on a cheerful tone. "I know what we'll do, Champo. You know how we've talked about people hearing things through the air that you don't even say out loud?"

He wriggled closer, laying his head against her shoulder. "Like that ASP you mean. That's what I did before when I thought about you. It worked, too, didn't it?" She felt his head nod against her in satisfaction.

"ESP. Right. We're going to use it now. Together. We'll be twice as strong."

"Okay. What do we do?"

"We're going to think about Mr. Link."

"How come him?" Andy coughed, and Courtney wrapped him tighter inside her sweater, hoping her own meager body heat would help warm him.

"Because one time I told him about our game, and about how you said you were hiding in a cave."

"So maybe he would remember?" Andy's little voice was hopeful.

"Maybe. If we think it hard enough. Okay?"

"Okay." Andy nodded again against her shoulder and took a deep breath. "I'll think, Auntie Court, but I'm scared and I'm so tired..." His voice drifted off and she moved slightly to make herself more comfortable. It looked as though it was going to be a one-signal ESP. She was tired too; neither she nor Link had slept much last night.

Was it really only a few hours ago that they had looked down on the lights of the city? It seemed at least a year. Think about me, Link, she telegraphed. But don't think about our conversation in the plane. Remember our talk on the island, about Andy's game. Open to me, please!

Above them, the storm raged. Though they were underground, Courtney could hear limbs cracking and falling, even once in a while the thump of a tree or large branch falling nearby. The growth on this incline was old, the tall pines ancient by any standards. How would anyone guess to comb this hill as she had? Unless her mental telepathy worked.

"Auntie Court?" mumbled Andy's sleepy voice, "I'm really hungry."

"Oh, of course you are. Just a minute." She dug out the Hershey bar that was not only slightly melted but now more than a little squashed by her falling on it. "Here. This candy's a little worse for wear, but it will hit your hungry spot."

"Oh, thanks! I never even had any breakfast.

Mom was sleeping and I was just going to come up here for a little while before she woke up." The sweet chocolate smell as he munched on the bar made Courtney's mouth water, too. She and Link had left Chicago in such as hurry that neither of them had eaten, either. Time enough for that later, if she and Andy ever got out of this godforsaken hole.

Andy finished the bar and snuggled back inside her sweater, coughing slightly. "That was good, Auntie Court. Now I'm thinking about Mr. Link. Are you?"

"I surely am." She was thinking his lips, his voice, his eyes, the strength of his arms, his gentleness as he said, "Don't talk. Don't move...I want you beyond speaking." I'm thinking, but about all the wrong things, she told herself. Stick to the subject at hand. Remember the conversation on the island, remember telling him about Andy's game.

But her remembrances of the island were far more interesting than the conversation they'd had, and time and again Courtney had to bring her thoughts back to signaling Lincoln Spencer about Andy's cave.

She felt Andy's body slump against her as he gave himself over to sleep. Then suddenly he jerked, gasping, struggling for breath, choking as he cried out, "I-I can't breathe!"

Courtney held him close, stroking his hair back from his forehead, crooning, "It's all right, Champo. You fell asleep. You just had a bad dream and it frightened you. We're okay. I won't let anything happen to you." She rocked him gently until his breathing eased. They would have to get out of this chilly hole before long or he would be in real trouble.

"Auntie Court, they will find us, won't they?" Though it was too dark to see his face, Courtney could picture the worried frown that was evident in his labored voice. "Won't somebody?"

Please God, yes, she thought, and soon, before Andy's frail body reacted as it had in the past. She pulled her sweater tighter around the both of them and said with false bravado, "They will, Champo. They will."

****

Judge Adam Burns, breathing laboriously, paced across and back, across and back, over the Persian carpeting in the elaborate study of his Lake Forest home. On the desk behind him were the corporation papers drawn up by Lincoln Spencer. Everything was in order except for one item: Lincoln's name was not included. He had refused the one-sixth interest.

Why?

Why would a struggling young lawyer who admittedly wanted the judges' backing and the backing of his party men for admission into Illinois politics deliberately leave himself out of a sixty-thousand dollar participation in a corporation formed by those men? Men that could put him on the political map?

The money was a gift, and they both knew it, though the other four men were unaware that Lincoln's share had actually been put up by the judge. It was a gift that included Georgie as collateral.

"You'll withdraw your backing unless I marry your daughter?" The judge remembered Lincoln's astonished expression as clearly as he had seen it on the afternoon Lincoln had incredulously asked the question. And the judge also remembered the way Lincoln's gaze had repeatedly returned to the winsome figure on the pier at Courtney's Sports when they had been out on the water.

Damn the man! Georgie wanted him; it would be so simple if he'd just accept. The judge didn't have a whole lot more time to get things settled for her. He stopped at the window onto the formal garden, his hands behind his back. The wind was so strong that even the low-planted flowers were tossing wildly. The worst storm in years up on the peninsula, they'd said on the news. He wondered how his old cottage was standing up; God, he missed that place.

He could understand Lincoln wanting to live in Door County. He'd spent most of his growing-up years there. If the judge didn't have Georgie to think of he'd have kept the cottage and moved there himself when he was finally off the bench. But no, she was a city girl from the start, and that was that.

"You could get an apartment, Georgie. I'd keep it up for you, you know."

"And sell this house? Daddy! Don't you like being surrounded by mother's things?"

As a matter of fact, he didn't. The house and everything in it reminded him too much, too often, of what he'd lost when Laura had withered away. He wanted Georgie to have that kind of a love, too. If she were married he could close the house, go anywhere. Lincoln would have been—still was—the perfect answer.

It was probably that dammed James woman. How she'd gotten into the picture was a puzzle, but it probably had something to do with that old busybody Amy Lane. It seemed half the stuff that ever went on in the Sister Bay area had her nose poked into it.

Well, he'd promised Georgie he'd take care of the James woman, and he would. He picked up the phone and dialed an investigator he'd used in the past when he'd needed fast background information for financial matters. "Get me everything you can on a woman named Courtney James...and quick. Use any means you have, but I want it yesterday."

The conversation was short and to the point. The judge put down the phone with a smile. In just a few hours he'd have found the woman's Achilles heel. It was always easy to buy somebody out, force somebody out, frighten somebody out. You just had to know what would hurt them the most.

Chapter Twenty-one

After following Courtney's directives of a hot bath and short rest, at Lisbet's insistence she and Jerry hurried downhill to the store, heads bent against the gusting wind and rain, ducking as lightning and thunder crackled and crashed too closely around them.

"I have to be near that phone, Jerry," Lisbet said. "I don't know what else I can do." Her eyes had pleaded with him. "I know you have to get back to Milwaukee, but won't you stay with me? Just until we find Andy?"

"You don't need to ask. Milwaukee can wait." His hand held hers tightly. "Silly girl. Of course I'll stay with you, Liss, until we've got him safely home. If anything happens to that kid—believe me, I understand what you're going through."

In the past few days Jerry had understood a lot of things about himself, some of them confusing, and one of the most interesting was that he reveled in the company of a dependent woman like Lisbet who wasn't so sure of herself and who needed, actually *wanted*, a man to lean on. She was so totally different from Courtney; it was hard to believe they were sisters.

Over dinner with Andy at the Yacht Club the night before, Lisbet had agreed the two were very much unlike. "She's the strong one, as if you don't know," Lisbet said. "I guess she had to be. She took over when our mother died, and no one could have done better. She's done way more than she should have to make my life the best it could have been, and she still does...bringing us here this summer, letting me feel important by helping in her store. She's given up so much for me over the years. She's wonderful, Jerry." Lisbet had smiled at him companionably over their dinner. I don't blame you for being in love with her."

"What's *in love* mean?" Andy had asked, forking up a crusty piece of fish and looking from one to the other for an answer as he chewed.

"Good question." Jerry grinned at Lisbet. "I've asked myself that a lot of times, and I think I'm finally beginning to know."

"Really?" Lisbet raised her eyebrows. "How so?"

"Really." Jerry had only hesitated a moment before reaching for her hand. "I don't deny I love Courtney. I always have, and I always will. She's been part of my life for a long time. But this is different." He reached across the table to cup her chin in his other hand. "I'm *in* love with you, Lisbet."

Andy was momentarily forgotten. "Me!" Lisbet's mouth opened in surprise as she raised her eyes to Jerry's, and the realization of what he said sank in. "In love with me!" she repeated. She hesitated. "But—"

"Don't say anything. Not now. Just know. I'll be around, whenever you need me."

"What about me?" asked Andy, looking from one to the other.

"And we're both in love with you, Squirt," grinned Jerry. "Now finish your dinner."

We have to find him, thought Jerry now as he and Lisbet hurried through the wet wind past Courtney's dark cabin toward the store. Andy had become the son that Jerry lost. These few days alone with him and Lisbet had been wonderful, giving him a perspective he'd never seen with Courtney in the picture. Now he understood what it was he needed

171

desperately, and in Lisbet and Andy he'd found the family he missed so much. And now, to think of losing Andy, too...Jerry couldn't let that thought into his mind. He pushed open the door to the brightly lit store but had to shoulder it closed against the wildly swirling wind that blew through the store, scattering papers and small items off the counter.

"Court!" Lisbet called, shaking off her wet scarf. "Any news?"

No answer.

"She must be in the stockroom." Lisbet opened the door to the back room, which was dark. She turned to Jerry, puzzled and angry. "How could she leave? She had to be here for the phone!" Lisbet ran to the desk and picked up the instrument. "It's dead!"

Jerry checked it, rattled it, tested it again. "She must have gone somewhere for a good reason. But wouldn't she have left a note?"

His voice was cut off as the door burst open, admitting a wet and worried Lincoln Spencer.

Jerry watched Lisbet run toward Link, her face alive with hope that turned to misery at the empty expression on his.

"Nothing." Exhausted, Lincoln sank down on a chair near the counter. I buzzed the whole shoreline, all the possibilities, fighting that damn wind and rain. Nothing...I hooked a ride from the airstrip." He looked around the room as he ran a hand through his dark, wet hair. "Where's Courtney?"

Lisbet wring her hands. "We don't know. She was to stay here by the phone but it's dead now. There's no way to communicate with the Coast Guard, or the police—" Her voice ended in a wail and she turned, sobbing, into Jerry's arms.

"Hold on, Liss," he said softly, pressing her head into his shoulder. "I'm here. It will be all right. Hold on."

Lincoln paced the floor. "Damn it! That crazy Courtney has gone out in this to look for him herself, I know it!"

Over Lisbet's head, Jerry questioned, "Where would she look?"

"If I only knew..." Link stopped in front of the window, watching the waves pound over the dock, their spray blowing all the way to the store and streaming in heavy rivulets down the windowpane. "She's out somewhere in this, maybe hurt...the little fool." He ran both hands through his unruly hair, talking aloud more to himself than to the others. "She knows that boy better than anybody does...they play some crazy imagination games..." He stopped suddenly, smacking his fist into an open palm. "That's it!"

Lisbet raised her head. "What?" She ran to Lincoln, pulling on his arm, pleading, "What, Link?"

"The game! Of course..."

"What game?" She shook his jacket sleeve. "What are you talking about?"

His eyes were darkly intense. "The game you played with you were kids, remember? Listen! We've got to comb the bluff up behind the cottages. Andy's up there, in some cave! I'm certain of it!"

"But...how do you know?" Lisbet's eyes shone with wary hope.

"I just do. Mitchell, get your coat on. Lisbet, maybe you should stay here. It's pretty rough out there and the storm hasn't let up. We'll bring him back."

"No. He's my son." Lisbet's small face was determined. "And there's no reason to stay here."

"Then come on."

Lincoln led the way up the hill to the area behind the cottages, holding back wet branches for the two following him until he was fifty feet or so in the thick underbrush up behind the cabins. His shoulders sagged. God, it all looked the same. Where to begin?

The wind suddenly whirled with hurricane force and above and to his left a large old pine fell, its heavily branched upper trunk nearly obliterating a large upturned root system as it thudded to the ground. A shudder went through Link's body at the unleashed violence around him and the certain knowledge that Courtney, soft, responsive, reluctantly loving Courtney, had to be somewhere near.

Link felt that as surely as if he could hear her calling his name, pulling him toward this hill. He had to find her, keep her safe. She said she believed in ESP, he thought, remembering vividly their island conversation about Andy's game. We'll see. Think of me, Courtney. Think! Lead me to you.

Link pointed across the bluff, raising his voice over the wind. "Try to make a straight line across the incline, Mitchell. Lisbet, too. I'll go up a little higher."

"Wait, Link. What are we looking for?" Lisbet shouted, waving her arm at the wooded incline. "There's nothing here!"

"There has to be. Somewhere on this bluff. A small opening to a hole or cave of some sort. Behind a big tree." He stared up at the branches that moved wildly against the grey sky and shivered in spite of his warm sweater and leather jacket. We have to find them before nightfall, he thought. They'll be frozen.

"A big tree," echoed Jerry. "Sure. Just one of a thousand. Okay, then, let's move!"

The thunder and roar of the wind above was constant, sucked into their dim underground prison by the force of the gale that determinedly swirled fresh damp air down into the earth's opening with vengeance. Now that her eyes had adjusted, Courtney could ascertain the faint light coming from where she had so stupidly slid down into the hole. The opening brightened with each flash of lightning, then dimmed again. Would this damned storm ever let up?

Cold and trying to ignore the increasing throbbing in her injured ankle, Courtney held Andy's slight, shivering body as close to her as she could. Her slicker and sweater weren't large enough to cover his cold bare legs. He must have grown six inches in this past month, and all between his hips and toes, she thought as she snuggled him close, hoping that if she could keep his torso warm, heated blood would pump to his extremities.

Andy's head nodded against her. At least he wasn't down here alone, and surely the storm would abate soon and help would come. At least she knew that their voices could reach outside—if there was anyone near enough to hear. After all, she'd heard Andy, even over the storm. They had shouted on a regular basis for some time after she'd fallen in with Andy, until both their voices were hoarse and it hurt to call. And finally, as Andy's asthma was aggravated by the effort and his fright, they'd stopped.

"We'd better just wait, Champo. Nobody is up there now, and we'll just make ourselves sick. Let's just keep warm and concentrate on thinking about Mr. Link." She didn't want Andy to overextend his frail physical abilities any more than he already had; his breathing already showed the damp cold was taking its toll.

"I like Mr. Link a lot, Auntie Court, and I am thinking about him." Andy's voice was muffled against her sweater. "But how do we know he's thinking about us?"

Good question. How did they know he hadn't

crashed against the bluff himself, down toward Horseshoe Bay? She could only hope. "He is, Andy. I just know he is."

Courtney leaned her head back against the solid rock behind her, sending all her mental energy to the tall, lean man, the very thought of whom turned her body into a mass of physical agitation. Just my luck, she thought wryly, to fall in love with someone I can't have. And who obviously doesn't want me except as a bed partner. Which, she reminded herself, she had certainly proved more than willing to be.

But...her mind wouldn't forget his tenderness at the same time she resented the fact that he could make love to her the way he did, and in the next breath show such concern for her sister when the phone rang. It was clear that sex and love were two different things. Probably Miss Georgie Burns of the voluptuous body was another of his sexual conquests. Surely he didn't see that one for her brains.

Courtney replayed the night on the island. He had said wonderful things—she was a goddess, she was beauty—but love? Had he even once mentioned the word? No. And last night, again. Nothing. Nothing but the wonder of his lips, his arms, the feel of his body on hers, taking, giving...

When they got out of this hole she would keep her life in order, as planned. No more Lincoln Spencer. She'd already told him that, and he had promised to leave it that way. "If that's the way you want it," he'd said.

A horrendous crack of lightning brightly illuminated every inch of their underground cavern. "No!" Courtney shrieked, clutching Andy in terror as simultaneous thunder shook the ground even as far below as they were. Immediately a new a frightening sound, a rending and tearing as though nature itself were breaking into a thousand pieces, reverberated through the air, followed by a tremendous thud that shook small pieces of rock loose onto their heads. Suddenly their small world was as pitch black as though they had been dropped into a bottle of ink and the noise of the storm seemed far away.

"What's happened, Auntie Court?" Andy cried, struggling against her as he came up from sleep. "It's all dark now!" His breath was shallow. She'd have to calm him or he would succumb to his ever-hovering asthma.

"It's all right, Champo. It's all right," she soothed him even as with a horrible sinking in her stomach Courtney realized that their only hope of escape, the small opening in the rock above, had just been completely covered by a fallen tree.

Chapter Twenty-two

"Well, what have you got?"

"Nothing."

"What do you mean, nothing?" Judge Adam Burns fixed the thin, sallow man across the desk with narrowed eyes as though he were studying some kind of insect specimen. "I know you didn't have much time, but there can't be nothing. Everybody's got some skeleton in a closet, something they prefer to keep hidden. Or something that means a great deal to them."

"You wanted quick service, and you got it. It was easy. I tell you, there's nothing. Courtney James is as clean as Ivory Soap. It's all there on one simple page. And, my expenses."

The Judge picked up the folder and mumbled aloud through the sparse information.

"Courtney James, nee Courtney Wilson. Parents deceased. One sister, Lisbet Grant, one nephew, Andrew John Grant. Married three years, no children, damn! Buyer, Ladd's Department Store, Milwaukee, until she bought the Sister Bay property this last spring. Husband killed in racing accident over a year ago. No court record, not even a traffic ticket, hell!" the judge exploded, slapping the papers down on the desk. "There's nothing I can use here!"

"That's what I said."

The judge sat back in his chair, fingertips tented together, his eyes closed momentarily as he brought up a phlegmy cough. "No close personal friends, male or better yet, female?"

"Not really. Jerry Mitchell, the driver, is a friend, but only that. She kept pretty much to herself. Just her sister. And the little kid. She dotes on the kid, I guess."

"I want her out of that store."

The sallow man pursed his lips and twisted his mouth. "How badly do you want her out?"

"Badly. I want her out of the picture for good."

The man shifted in his chair, looking slyly at the judge. "You could burn her out."

"You're joking."

"Not unless you are. You want her out? She didn't have enough money to buy outright, and she's on a contract until the down payment's fulfilled. She probably hasn't got enough insurance to rebuild or restock. She's put herself in hock for some clothing for the winter and next season..." The man raised his brows, shrugged and made a distasteful sucking noise through his teeth. "Just a thought."

The silence in the room was only broken by the Judge's labored breathing. You know I couldn't..." He was silent for a moment before he pushed himself heavily to his feet. "I'll send your check. We never had this conversation."

"Have we ever had any conversation?" The man's mouth screwed into a half-snort.

"Never."

"See 'ya, Judge. Call anytime." The man tipped his hat as he slipped through the open door, unaware of Georgie's slight figure standing motionless just around the corner.

****

Link, Jerry and Lisbet trudged and stumbled back and forth, back and forth across the rugged incline, fighting the storm every inch of the way, stopping every few seconds to call and listen, a repeat of Courtney's earlier performance over the same terrain.

"Courtney! Andy!" Their fragile voices were torn from their mouths and whirled up through the madly dancing branches, lost to the storm.

No answer. Toward evening the sky was even darker. It seemed to Link that they had been searching forever. Was it only hours ago that he and Courtney had been together in Chicago? Courtney, Courtney, he pleaded silently. Hear me, lead me! But there was just more wind, more rain, jagged lightning, thunder, falling branches.

An hour later they had covered under half of the bluff when Lisbet, tears running down her rain-wet face, struggled over a downed branch and fell face down in rotting wood and pine needles. Link's reaction to help was stopped by Mitchell's shout of "Liss!" as Jerry jumped over a leaf-filled ravine and hurried to her.

Link watched Mitchell tenderly brush Lisbet's sodden hair back from her forehead. He held her shivering body close to his chest, protecting her from the elements that seemed determined to drain away her last bit of resolve to find her son.

"I can't, Jerry," she sobbed. "I can't move any more. I want to but my legs won't cooperate."

"They don't have to," Jerry said decisively, and shouted to Lincoln, who now doggedly continued to fight his way around and through the heavy, wet underbrush. "I'm taking Liss back, Spencer. She's exhausted." At Lincoln's wave of understanding, Jerry added, "I'll be right back!" and picked Lisbet up as though she weighed nothing. He started downhill, her head rolling tiredly against his shoulder with every lurching step.

"I'm taking you to your cottage, dear," he murmured into her ear. "Lisbet, can you hear me?"

She nodded, too spent to answer aloud.

"And then I'm coming back up here."

Lisbet nodded again.

"If Andy's here, we'll find him."

She opened her dark-circled blue eyes and looked gratefully up at him. "I love you, Jerry," she said, and closed her eyes.

****

Lincoln rested wearily against a wind-whipped tree trunk and watched them go, dawning recognition of the newly-formed bond between the two of them writing approval all over his face. Mitchell's obvious interest in Lisbet removed him from any hold on Courtney's life. It would only remain now for Link to convince her that her Capital F future and his own were one and the same. And, he thought wryly, to kiss goodbye to any future for himself in Illinois politics.

It puzzled him that Courtney had pushed him so hard toward her sister. Lisbet was cute and sometimes funny, but she wasn't Courtney James, and she wasn't for him.

Courtney. His heart reached out to her in the storm; she had to be here, he could almost feel her nearness. The remembrance of her smooth, silky body in his arms sent an ache through his loins. If anything happened, if he couldn't hold her again... He'd been stupid, not telling her he loved her, but he wanted her to put away her resentment of him and his unexpected, unwanted position in her life first. He wanted her to reaffirm what she'd unknowingly murmured to him as she fell asleep on the island. He could almost hear her soft voice, feel her long honey-blond hair as it had been spread across his passion-warmed chest: "You have my heart, Lincoln Spencer...for the rest of my life."

He brushed his wet hair back from his forehead and forged ahead across the bluff. And now, what if it was too late? Too long out in this weather and pneumonia could be a killer no matter how ordinarily healthy a person was.

Sighing, he sank down on the trunk of an enormous, newly-fallen tree and dropped his head in his hands, remembering Courtney's fury at him for the empty gas tank in her boat, which, he was sure, had been Georgie's contribution. Had she wanted to make Courtney look bad, her boat out of gas for an unwitting renter? What a childish, silly thing to do and he smiled at its most pleasant consequence, what a backfire!

He wearily rubbed the soaking back of his neck. It had been a long night without much sleep, a tension-filled trip in the small plane, an exhausting and often frightening search over the wind-whipped water near the bluffs, and if Courtney and Andy weren't found soon it would be dark and there would be no use in searching until morning.

Lincoln shivered, chilled to the bone. The temperature seemed to be dropping at an alarming rate. Wherever Courtney and Andy were, for he was sure they were together, he prayed they were warm and dry.

****

Shivering in the damp darkness, Courtney and Andy huddled close, conserving what body heat they had left.

"I don't feel so good, Auntie Court."

She quickly pressed her palm to his small, heated forehead. No doubt about it, he would be a very sick little boy if they didn't get out soon. The storm sounded less wild now because of the fallen tree that so effectively cut off any light and sound, but she was sure from the thunder that unceasingly shook the ground that it would still be useless to shout.

Andy stirred against her.

"Shall we make up a story, Champo? We're good at that."

"No. I don't feel like it."

"Then how about a song? That will cheer us up. We know some good ones." Anything to distract him.

"Maybe. If you sing it. Do you 'member that silly song about the ol' woman that ate the fly?" Andy whispered.

"Sure do."

"Will you sing it? It makes me laugh."

What she wouldn't give to hear his happy giggle. Could she remember all the words? "There was an old woman who swallowed a fly," she began to sing softly. "I don't know why—" her voice cracked and she blinked back tears and cleared her throat before continuing, "—she swallowed a fly. I guess she'll die."

She felt him turn his face up to hers. "Will we die, Auntie Court?"

Though she couldn't see his dear little freckled face, she pictured the worry on it. "No way, Champo. Come on, sing with me. Okay? Here we go, spider's next. Ready? There was an old woman...come on!...who swallowed a spider. It wiggled and wiggled and wiggled," she tickled his thin little ribs as she sang, "inside her."

Andy's high little voice joined hers. "She swallowed the spider to catch the fly. I guess she'll die!" Andy started to giggle, getting into the spirit of the song. Together their voices filled the dark as they swayed back and forth, back and forth, singing louder and louder.

At least it's getting his mind off their predicament, Courtney thought, and in addition expending some energy to warm them both.

"I know an old woman who swallowed a bird...how absurd, to swallow a bird!" they sang. "She swallowed a bird to catch the spider, that wiggled and wiggled and wiggled inside her." And Andy, as he always did in this part of the verse, flapped his elbows and cheeped loudly, "Tweet!

Tweet!"

Above them the wind abated for only a moment but it was just enough as a tired, wet and discouraged Lincoln Spencer waited for Jerry's return. In the momentary lull a thin little voice filtered up through the thick pine branches of the fallen tree on which Link rested.

"Tweet! Tweet!"

Was he hearing things? Surely no bird actually said 'tweet!' And they certainly didn't tweet in the midst of the worst storm in years. He cocked his head and picked up faint voices, "...swallowed a bird to catch the spider."

Elation surged through him. "Courtney!" he shouted, jumping to his feet. "Courtney! Where the hell are you!"

"...know why she swallowed the fly. I guess she'll die."

Before they could start another verse he was tearing at branches, pulling them away in a frenzy that gave him nearly superhuman strength. "I'm coming, Courtney," he muttered. "Just keep on singing."

Below him, the song went on for Andy's benefit. "I know an old woman who swallowed a goat—" Courtney broke off singing as a new sound hit her ear and suddenly faint light showed above them. "Listen, Champo! Listen!"

"Courtney! Andy!"

"It's Mr. Link!" Andy cried. "He did come!"

She hugged Andy, tears of relief flowing as she got to her feet, favoring her hurt ankle as she looked up toward the opening, calling with joy in her voice, "Here, Link! Down here! Oh, I knew you'd come!"

"Don't stop talking! I haven't found an opening yet!"

"All right! Mary had little lamb, its fleece was white..."

184

"Thank God, I've found it." Lincoln's voice came clearly now, echoing into their cavern. "But I can't see a thing. What will I need to get you out of there? Is it deep?

"About ten-twelve feet, I think."

His voice was husky with relief. "Are you okay? Is Andy?"

"Yes. But hurry, Link! He's chilled to the bone."

How like her not to admit that she was, too. He could hear the tremors in her voice. "I'll need a rope. And a light."

"I've got a light. It's dim, but it works."

"Keep singing, Sweetheart. I'll be right back."

Suddenly there was only the sound of the storm.

"He's gone, Auntie Court! He's gone!" Andy turned his face into her sweater.

"But he'll be back in no time. Come on, Andy! We'll be out of here before you know it!"

Link had called her Sweetheart! She hugged Andy close and their voices joined together. "I know an old lady who swallowed a goat...just opened her throat and swallowed a goat." The silly song rose triumphantly above the wind and rain.

Chapter Twenty-three

A few minutes later Lincoln was back with Jerry and Lisbet, carrying a saw for the large branch that so effectively blocked the entrance, and a rope long enough, he hoped, to reach them down in their damp prison.

He tried to squeeze his broad shoulders into the opening, but didn't fit. "I can't get in," he called, raising his voice to carry over the storm. "I'll toss the rope."

"Okay. Got it!" Courtney tied it loosely across Andy's small chest under his arms. She gave him a quick kiss and a pat on his bottom. "There you go, Champo! See you upstairs. Pull, Link! Andy's coming up!"

She watched his thin legs slide up over the top of their prison, thanking God for Link's memory of their island conversation.

"Next!" The dirt-covered rope snaked down to her and she looped it around her slicker under her arms, kicking her way up the dirt and stone wall as Link and Jerry hauled her slowly to the opening. The last few feet on the short incline to the open air were even more muddy than they had been when she slithered in, and her slicker slid over them with ease. The combined strengths of Jerry's and Link's pulling popped her out onto the wet, leafy ground. She smiled wearily up at her rescuers. "Th-thanks," she whispered through chattering teeth, though the wind and rain were a welcome replacement for the damp, dark cold inside the cave.

"You're freezing!" Link said, pulling her up. She stumbled slightly, favoring her ankle. "And you're hurt!"

"Only a l-little," she answered.

"How bad is it?" His eyes were dark with concern.

"I'll be fine. It's only a twist. Really."

A few feet away Lisbet knelt, crooning to Andy as she wrapped him in a warm woolen blanket from her cottage and he squeaked in an excited little voice, "Auntie Court found me, Mom! And then Mr. Link found us both."

"I know, baby. Your Auntie Court is something else." Lisbet's eyes thanked Courtney more than any words could have as she rocked her son against her breast. "Let's get you in a hot tub right away."

"I'll carry him." Jerry picked up the blanketed child. "Let's go, Liss." They started picking their way down the now nearly dark hill toward Lisbet's cottage.

Courtney turned luminous eyes up to Link. "You remembered! I was sure you would. Andy was beginning to show a fever, and I was so worried!" She managed a small smile as she struggled to move but her face blanched as her twisted ankle buckled under her. Link caught her up in strong arms before she fell.

"I can walk. Put me down!"

"Not a chance. I can see from here your ankle's swollen."

"I told you, it's just a twist."

"Just a twist can be more painful than a break. Be quiet."

"Yes, sir." She was too exhausted to argue, and shut her eyes, resting her head on his sturdy shoulder as he slowly made his uneven way down the hill. She was so relieved to have Andy safe. Now if only she could get warm.

"The storm's not so bad now," she murmured against his leather jacket. In spite of her resolve to be strong, at least until she could get into her own hot tub, she was fading fast. Link's arms were heavenly around her. If only they could be permanently hers.

"Nothing is so bad now, Love," he answered. "Nothing." He held her tightly as a chill shuddered through her body.

"Link." Had he called her *Love*? She forgot what she intended to say, and let her mind fall into oblivion until she felt herself lowered into a soft chair and opened her eyes.

"Why, we're in Amy's cottage! Take me home!" She attempted to rise but he firmly pushed her back into the chair.

"Nothing doing. I want you where you can get warm as quickly as possible, and this fire will do it. And correction, please, it's my cottage now." He touched a match to the laid fire and in a matter of seconds crackling flames blazed warmth through the whole room.

Link knelt in front of her, gently untying her sodden tennis shoes. He eased them off, examining her swollen ankle tenderly. She winced.

"You're right, it's not broken. But your feet are ice. And so is the rest of you. Off with those clothes."

"I'm fine. The fire is wonderful. Just let me warm up a little." But her chattering teeth gave her away.

"Don't be so damned independent. If I have to beat you, I will. Stand here by the fire."

He meant it, and she was too tired to resist. He pulled her to her feet and gently unsnapped her slicker, pulled off her damp sweater, slacks and blouse. As each article was removed she felt her body act on its own, responding to the welcome warmth of his fire and his tender touches that seemed to smooth away her goosebumps at the same time they divested her of clothing.

"No!" she said as he pulled her toward him to unhook her bra.

"Don't argue. I'm not seducing you. You're damp right to the skin." She struggled for a second, but only a second, as he deftly undid the article and then slid her soaked pantyhose to the floor. I'm dreaming, she thought. Could this be Courtney James, standing nude in front of a crackling fireplace in Lincoln Spencer's cottage? I was never going to be alone with him again...and...

Her mind was fuzzy. Her body ached for his touch but he was all business.

He pulled a heavy woven Indian blanket from the couch in the corner and wrapped her completely in it, settling her in the comfortable overstuffed chair next to the fireplace. A loud whistle from the kitchen startled her, but he only said, "Just a minute," and was back in moment with a mug of hot buttered rum. "This will help the inside. Now I'll help the outside."

He brought a large terry towel and a blow dryer from the bathroom and methodically began to brush and dry her long, bedraggled hair as she sipped from the heavy mug.

"Delicious," Courtney murmured, savoring both the warm drink and his solicitation. "What have I done to deserve this wonderful treatment?"

"Just been a heroine is all. A slightly dumb one for not telling anyone where you went. I was nearly out of my mind."

"But I left a note. On the counter."

"We didn't find it. It must have blown away when we opened he door. But all's well that ends well, as they say. You have lovely hair, Miz James."

His deep grey eyes met hers over the rim of her hot drink. They seemed to speak a whole library's worth, but she wasn't sure just what it was they said. She wanted to fall into his arms, into his bed, to wake up with him beside her as she had this morning.

"Link?" What was he doing here taking care of her when now of all times Lisbet must need his support, his care?

"No talk. Just drink, and enjoy."

Enjoy. It seemed he was always telling her to enjoy. The night on the lake, last night in the tower. Was it really only last night? It seemed like eons ago.

Firm hands pulled her to a straight sitting position, and, kneeling in front of her, methodically began to rub her down, starting with her neck, her arms, her back and torso. He took his time, gently rubbing each breast slowly, then again around her lower back, down her hips, her thighs, deftly manipulating her muscles to spread the fire's warmth through her body, down her legs and ankles.

The warmth that spread didn't all come from the fire. He rubbed her cold feet, moving and stroking, manipulating each toe individually, finally tucking them into a pair of his own warm fur-lined slippers.

"There!" He pulled the blanket solidly around her and sat back on his haunches. "Warm now?"

Was she! Her body reacted with desire that peaked her breasts, centered low in her stomach and turned her thoughts upside down. What was she doing here? Naked in a blanket with this man's fur slippers her only clothing? Surreptitiously she glanced below his waist and noted that his body wasn't totally unaffected by her vulnerability. But that was just biology.

"Wonderfully warm, thanks to you." Did he have any idea how she felt about him? How she wanted him? *I won't see you alone again*, she'd said, but here she was. And here she wanted very much to be.

"Finish your drink."

"I will. It's the answer to a cold and hungry stomach's prayer."

"And me?"

"You, too. I can't thank you enough."

"Yes, you can. Try."

Her startled eyes met his. What did he mean? Another sensual round that would be wonderful at the time and end with her guilty knowledge that he would never be hers? He had to be aware that her body responded alarmingly to his touch. Did he know the temptation to throw herself in his arms was almost more than she could bear? Did he feel it, too?

"Shouldn't you—" she began, but he had risen on his knees and his mouth was so close to hers that she could feel his warm breath against her face.

"Shouldn't I what?"

She turned away from his penetrating eyes, his lips. "Shouldn't you check on Lisbet?"

"Jerry's with her."

"I know, but..."

"You silly goose. Jerry is going to be with her for the rest of her life, if I'm any judge of things." His lips were on her earlobe.

Courtney was immobile for a moment as what he said sank into her exhausted brain. Then she pushed back to stare at him, her mouth open, her eyes sparkling stars. "Lisbet and Jerry!"

"Lisbet and Jerry."

"Are you sure?"

"Is the Pope Catholic?" He grinned, devouring her face with his eyes. The next move was hers.

Courtney sank back in the chair, letting her eyes touch every inch of his face. She didn't have to stand aside for Lisbet. Not any more. She could tell Lincoln Spencer how much she loved him. "Link." She leaned toward him.

He waited.

"Link." Could he see her heart in her eyes?

She shivered but not with cold as reached to slide the blanket down off her shoulders, rubbing his warm hands slowly down her arms, brushing against the responsive peaks of her creamy breasts ever so lightly. "You're lovely," he said. "Do you know how lovely?"

But he's never said he loves me, she thought, catching her lower lip between her teeth. And I want so badly to hear that from him. She shut her eyes.

"You were going to say something?" His hands were on her shoulders, mesmerizing her, pulling her toward him. "Go ahead, say it."

Her face flushed a becoming pink. "I-I..."

The door burst open and a cold wet draft swept through the cozy room. Courtney jumped and quickly pulled the blanket up around her shoulders, but not soon enough.

"I'm here, Linky! At last!" cried Georgie Burns, pulling a wet scarf from her bright blond head. "This storm is terrib—" Her breathless little-girl voice stopped in mid-sentence as its owner stopped and stared at the tableau silhouetted in front of the fire. In a split second, her tone was icy and the expression on her face changed to livid anger. "But what the hell is this...this fishstore person doing here!"

Chapter Twenty-four

"Excuse me. I seem to be in the wrong place at the wrong time," Courtney said stiffly, rising. She pulled the blanket tightly around her shoulders, chastising herself for being a fool. It seemed obvious that Lincoln Spencer had expected an evening rendezvous with Georgie Burns. "I'll be going now."

Mustering all the dignity she could while dressed only in a blanket and too-large fur slippers that flapped with every step, she limped past a furious Georgie to the door. "Thank you for your help," she enunciated to an astonished Spencer. "I'll see myself out."

"Like hell you will!" He was on his feet, but she was gone out into a whoosh of wind and rain, the wild-patterned blanket flapping behind her, his fur slippers sliding crazily over the muddy path.

"Don't you dare leave this room, Lincoln Spencer!" Georgie screeched, rushing to slam the door and stand between him and the way out. She stamped her little elegantly-booted foot as he reached around her for the doorknob. "Don't you dare! You can't! Daddy said—"

Lincoln stood ramrod straight, looking at her with cold, narrowed eyes, then stepped menacingly toward her, his large hands making fists at his sides. His voice was low and deadly quiet. "Your daddy said what?"

Georgie shrank against the doorframe. "Why are you looking at me like that? And why do you sound so mad?" She lifted her chin. "Daddy said—"

He took another step toward her. "Go on. Say it!"

She backed up again. "I don't want to." Georgie put on her prettiest pout and looked up at him from under long, darkened lashes. "It's all right, Linky. I know you weren't doing anything with that person."

"*That person* is Courtney James. And yes, I most certainly was doing something with her. Something important that you most rudely interrupted. What are you doing here?"

She tossed her wet blond pageboy arrogantly. "You knew I'd come back." But her expression had lost its assurance as she tried to read the unfamiliar look on his face. "I-I know I shouldn't have walked out on you last night. Daddy said—"

'Spit it out. Your daddy said what?" Spencer folded his arms across his chest and impaled her with a look that reduced her to a bug under a microscope. "And wipe that silly pout off your face. That cute baby stuff won't work on me any more, Georgie. God knows why it ever did. We're through. T.H.R.O.U.G.H! Got it?"

"But Linky, you know we're engaged!" She put a red-tipped hand on his sleeve and managed to squeeze a recalcitrant tear out of each painted eye.

"Oh? I don't remember anything like that."

"But we are! Daddy said we'd get married! Why do you think he put you in his corporation, and he got you the backing for office?" Her mascara was running down her cheeks now and mingling with an overabundance of rouge blush. She looked like a bedraggled clown. "He said he had it all fixed!"

"Well, Georgie, this time your daddy was wrong. Now, get out."

Her shoulders drooped for only a moment before she squared them. "You'll be sorry, Lincoln Spencer." But her chin quivered as she pulled open the door and attempted to make a dignified exit into the storm. "You and th-that fishstore person! Really sorry! You'll see!"

****

Once outside, tears of anger and embarrassment mixed with the rain on Courtney's face as she hobbled toward her own cabin. "Damn him!" she muttered. And she had been about to make a fool of herself, throw herself bodily into his arms.

Thank heaven for Georgie's timing. Another two minutes and I'd have been spraddled on the floor offering everything I have to someone who can't see beyond a fluffhead with a voluptuous little body and a daddy with a Lincoln town car, unlimited credit with American Express and political clout. Me? I was nothing more than a good toss when circumstances threw us together, that's all.

She stomped on one foot and limped on the other up to her porch, pulling the wayward wind-whipped blanket around her as best she could. She reached for her key hidden over the sill and pushed open the door to a cold, damp cabin that smelled musty from being closed up for the past few days. She locked the dead bolt behind her.

Courtney flipped a lighted match into the laid fireplace and threw the sodden blanket on the floor. She kicked off Lincoln's muddy slippers and hopped into the bathroom where she slammed the door so hard the window rattled. She turned the hot water on full force and climbed into the tub, shutting her eyes as the water rose around her.

Andy was safe. That was what mattered. As far as the rest of her life, for all she cared right now she might as well lie down and drown.

****

Georgie ran blindly up the gravel road to the town car, spun its wheels with a stomp on the gas pedal and headed blindly back toward the hotel. Her father would be there and she'd tell him what

195

happened. He'd said he'd take care of that James person, and he'd always done what Georgie wanted him to. He'd get that woman out of the picture somehow, and then Lincoln would be hers again.

Hers for good. They'd have a townhouse in Chicago and if he wanted to have a place up in Door County for weekends that was all right, too. But not here. Not in Sister Bay. She'd make him get rid of that musty little cottage and they'd get another place, maybe on the other side of the Peninsula. It wouldn't take long to convince him once she had the chance, a few kisses, and whatever else it took. He was as susceptible to sex as any other man. She'd handled him before, and now, with Daddy's help, everything would be just fine.

She squealed to a stop in their parking space. The wind hadn't lessened any but finally the rain had stopped coming down in sheets. Though it still sprinkled, the heavy clouds were breaking up. As she got out of the car she looked up to see a small sliver of the waning moon appear over the still wildly tossing waters of Green Bay.

Things were going to be all right. As soon as Linky cooled down and remembered who could do him the most good.

She slammed open the door to their rooms, but the judge was nowhere to be seen. Probably playing cards with those frightful old widows. She went unsuccessfully searching through the communal rooms for him, still fuming at the nerve of Lincoln to have that—that woman!—in his cottage. And with no clothes on! The more Georgie thought about it the angrier she got.

Daddy was wrong, Lincoln had said. But in all her years she couldn't remember her daddy being wrong. Sometimes it just took him a little bit longer to be right. He'd said they'd get rid of Courtney James. He'd even had his investigator look into her past. Georgie remembered the conversation she'd overheard between the two.

Where was the judge, anyway? Probably playing poker with those old cronies of his, and if that was so, who could even guess when he'd come home? Disconsolate, Georgie went back up to their rooms, poured herself a half-tumbler from the judge's good Scotch and swallowed it straight. It burned all the way down but it warmed her and she felt better. She poured herself a second.

Georgie plunked down on a chair, glass in hand, and stared out the window toward the turbulent grey waters of the Bay. She wanted Lincoln Spencer and if the only way to get him was to get rid of the James woman—Georgie's eyes narrowed as she reached inside her mind for something—what was it she'd overheard her father's investigator say? Burn her out!

Georgie swallowed the rest of the Scotch and poured herself a third glass. She downed that, too, thinking as clearly as she could before she pulled on her dark raincoat and tied a matching scarf over her blond head.

Sometimes things just couldn't wait. Sometimes Daddy was just too slow.

****

Courtney leaned back and wearily closed her eyes, neck deep in her hot bath, her aching body soothed by mounds of fragrant suds that smelled great but didn't do a whole lot for her mental state. She deliberately and repeatedly put the last hour out of her mind, but its events popped back in as fast as she threw them out.

The man was like a drug. His eyes, his arms, his tender hands...she snorted aloud, flipping a pile of suds halfway up the bathroom wall. She was probably only one of a dozen, or more, who'd succumbed to his virile charms at one time or another. He certainly was no novice at making love. The assured way he had so easily brought her to him on the island...and in Chicago. She shook her head, angry at herself. What had happened to that oh-so-independent Courtney James who started the summer so blithely in charge of her business and her life? Ever since their first meeting on the shore Lincoln Spencer had turned her world topsy-turvy.

Courtney lathered a soft terry washcloth and scrubbed her face until it hurt. Then with an exclamation, she threw the soapy cloth into the water so hard gobs of suds splatted on the wall and onto the red rug on the floor.

"Who cares!" she fumed. "Who the hell cares!"

What a day! She glanced at the now dark window...and what a night. What a false sense of elation, to know that Jerry and Lisbet cared for each other, that Jerry had found another interest, and that Lisbet really didn't want Lincoln after all.

And what a fool she'd almost made of herself, so ready to declare her love, forgetting completely about the man's ever-ready paramour, if that was what Georgie Burns was. Certainly she had some kind of hold on him; she'd not hesitated to burst into his cottage without knocking. And he'd said nothing. Evidently he didn't mind.

Mind! He was a normal male, and it seemed he enjoyed every minute of the baby-faced beauty. Courtney remembered the scene near the dock when Georgie's silky leg openly rubbed against his...and his willingness to squire the blond shopping, and to lunch with her obese, wheezing, doting father.

A furious pounding on her cottage door shattered her thoughts. She ignored it. The door was securely locked, and if he wanted his slippers and his damn blanket he could find them on her porch in the morning.

"Courtney! Open up!"

"Go to hell, Lincoln Spencer," she muttered and sank into the bath water far enough to cover her ears. "Go back to your blond."

The pounding went on, and she continued to ignore it. Finally it stopped and she heard heavy footsteps go down her porch steps.

She listened for a few more seconds, then said aloud, "Good riddance," though she didn't really feel it. What does a woman do, she asked herself, when she's fallen hopelessly in love, as they say in the romance novels, and it really is hopeless? Not once had he said he loved her.

Suddenly a deep, husky voice filled the little bathroom. "We didn't finish our conversation."

"Oh!" She jumped, sloshing water over the side of the tub, and stared up at her bathroom window which had silently slid open to frame Lincoln Spencer's dark head.

"You were about to tell me something, I believe," he said, leaning comfortably over the windowsill on crossed arms, "before we were so rudely interrupted."

She unconsciously covered her breasts with her arms, even though they were under the suds on the surface of her bath water. "Get out of here, y-you window peeker!"

"Not a chance. I like the view. But it is wet out here. Mind if I step in?" He calmly put one foot through the window, then another as her eyes widened in disbelief.

Damn! Why hadn't she repaired that screen instead of just taking it off when it rusted through? "You're trespassing!" she accused through clenched teeth. "I'll call the police."

It was a tight squeeze for him to get his broad shoulders through the window, but he accomplished it. "From your bathtub? Besides, you don't even have a phone."

Courtney stared at the ceiling. "Don't tell me your friendly fluff has already left you, when she was so anxious to get to you!"

"My friendly fluff—your words, not mine—has indeed gone," he said calmly. "She was never invited, in case you care. Want your back scrubbed?"

"No!" She cared, all right, but she wasn't going to tell him how much. "Please," she pleaded softly. "Just go away."

"As I said, we haven't finished our conversation." He sat on the edge of the tub and fished up the washcloth. "And it was just getting interesting. Lean forward."

Courtney deliberately lay back against the tub and drew her lips into a straight line. "If you came for your blanket and slippers, they're by the door." She didn't look at him.

"That's not what I came for." He crooked his finger under her chin and forced her to face him. "And you know it. Good God!" he gasped, "What in the world!" He stared at the floor by the bathroom door for a second before he jumped up to pull it open and was immediately enveloped in a cloud of black pine smoke that rolled into the room.

"What!" Courtney was up out of the tub in a flash, grabbing a towel to throw around her. "Oh, good grief, the fireplace! I forgot to open the damper!"

Holding his breath, Link bolted across the room through heavy layers of billowing smoke and jerked on the lever to open the flue. The smoke began to clear slowly as the draft pulled it up through the chimney.

"Whew! I thought for a minute there the whole place was on fire!" He shook his head. "You do seem to get yourself into all sorts of trouble. What would you do without me?" He grinned, observing her slim figure under the less than ample towel. "And you're freezing again. Get some clothes on, will you please? You're very distracting, undressed like that."

She stood her ground, though she was shivering badly. "Look, let's just call it a day. I'm very grateful for all you've done in rescuing Andy and me. I know we would have both had pneumonia if you hadn't found us before dark. But I really just want to fall into bed and sleep for a week. Okay?"

"Only if I fall in with you." He stepped toward her. "Now, either get some clothes on so we can talk rationally, or I'm going to do something drastic." He took two more steps.

He meant it. Courtney made a face and slammed the bedroom door. She pulled on clean underclothes and woolen slacks, a soft sweater, and warm knee socks. Sturdy walking oxfords gave her the feeling of being able to stand securely on her own two feet. Her hair that had been piled on top of her head for her bath had come down, and she took her own sweet time running a brush through it, leaving it to fall loosely down her back. She spent as long as she could in dressing until there was an authoritative knock on her door accompanied by, "Come out or I'm coming in!"

She came out, slowly. "This is under protest, you understand."

He whistled softly. "Protest or not, as I was saying earlier, you really are very lovely." His eyes were saying more.

She looked away, fanning her hand in front of her nose. "Phew! That smoke is awful. Shouldn't it have cleared by now?"

"Yes, but I don't think it's coming from here. It must be blowing from someone else's fireplace up the way. Smells odd, though, doesn't it? The wind is still crazy even though the rain has finally stopped. It's clearing."

"Let's see! Is it really?" Courtney walked to her

front window to look out over the bay. "What a storm! And what a nightmare we've had! Thank God it's over."

Then she caught her breath and whirled to face him, her face ashen. "Link! The store's on fire!"

Chapter Twenty-five

Georgie Burns tossed back her head and laughed aloud into the wind as she tossed a second flaming wad of twisted newspaper into the window she'd smashed on the dark north side of Courtney's Sports. There was a pile of canvas or something that looked like it in the corner right under the window. It was hard to see just what there was in that storeroom, but surely something in there would burn.

Her thinking was more than a little fuzzy and she had trouble keeping her balance in the still-gusting wind. She gave a ladylike burp and giggled aloud. Shouldn't have helped herself to quite so much of Daddy's Scotch, but what the hell. Sometimes you just need a little courage to take things into your own hands.

She stood on tiptoes and nearly clapped her hands as the lighted paper fell right where she wanted it. There! That ought to take care of that fishstore person!

Georgie had planned it perfectly. Every phone for miles was out of order; no one could call the fire department. Even wet from the storm, this old wooden building would go up like tinder. Nobody would get hurt, but that James woman would have to go back where she came from, and then—Georgie laughed out loud again—then Linky would forget about her and get his mind back on the right track.

Why wasn't the damn store starting to burn? Would she have to light another paper? She peeked

203

in, holding her breath, as a thin trail of smoke, then a finger of flame crept up the side of the wall and grew larger, fanning out to lick at some fish net hanging near the window, then flickering with hungry little tongues across the dry pine floor toward some cans near the wall.

Fascinated at how fast the fire spread, Georgie stood mesmerized at the window, watching the flames mount to follow along the wooden wall toward the other side of the room. Yes, it was going just right. Georgie smiled. She'd leave in just a minute, once she was sure there was no doubt the whole old building would burn to the ground.

Courtney was out of her cottage door in a moment with Lincoln Spencer right behind her.

"Courtney! Stop!" He caught her halfway down the hill. "It's no use with this wind!"

She looked up at him, her long hair blowing around her shoulders, anguish written all over her face. "I've got to do something!"

"No! Don't go any closer!" He pulled her back against him, only a second before an explosion ripped the whole north side of the storeroom off the building, shooting flames in every direction.

"The gasoline!" he shouted. "My God! You could have been killed!"

She turned her face into his shoulder, and he held her as she wept.

Judge Burns checked his watch as he entered his empty room, expecting Georgie to be waiting for him. Come to think of it, his car hadn't been in its regular parking space. Perhaps she'd gone down to see if Lincoln was at his cottage. He poured himself a nightcap, frowning as he sniffed the used glass next to the bottle on the table. It wasn't like Georgie to drink Scotch. She didn't really like the taste, and it usually went right to her head.

He settled himself in a chintz-covered chair with a mystery paperback. She'd be along soon, wherever she was, or—he chuckled aloud—if Lincoln was up at his place maybe she wouldn't be back at all before morning.

He lifted his head momentarily at the far-away wail of a fire siren, recrossed his legs more comfortably and went back to his book, thinking what bad weather it was to fight a fire, with the wind still blowing so wildly across the Bay.

With the complications of a downed tree behind Lincoln's car and no phone available, it was more than a half hour before he could summon the fire department. The still wild wind along with the rest of the stored oil and gasoline had made short work of the whole old wooden-shingled building in spite of its rain-soaked outer shell. There was no possibility of saving the store; in less than an hour Courtney's Sports was leveled, but in spite of the whirling wind, the torrential rain that had soaked the area kept the flames from spreading up the wooded hill to the old pines and the cottages.

From the shelter of Lincoln's arms Courtney looked blankly at the slickered fireman who was shining a large torch on a small, twisted and blackened figure crumpled against a tree trunk some thirty feet north of the smoking ruins that had been Courtney's Sports. Only a tumble of bright hair was recognizable above the charred clothing.

"B-but what was she doing here?" Courtney asked in a dazed voice.

"We don't have any idea, Miss. Did you know her?"

****

Lincoln Spencer's soot-blackened face was weary as, hours later, he handed Courtney a much-needed cup of strong, black coffee at the wooden table in his cottage kitchen. "Things are under control here, now. I've got to go to Judge Burns. Will you be all right?"

She nodded, picking at a piece of ash on her sweater sleeve. "I'm so sorry. She must have been coming back to see you."

"Walking along the shore?" He shook his head. "I doubt it. I don't know...God, to die like that..."

Courtney raised a tired face to his. "I'm so sorry," she said again. "Her poor father. I-I guess this closes a chapter, doesn't it? For her, for me." Courtney closed her eyes. "Another chapter closed by fire...first Ronnie, now the store...sorry. I'm babbling." She was quiet for a moment. "Everything I own—and owe for—was in that building except my own clothes."

"But the cottages are safe, and thank God we weren't nearer to the building when it blew. When I think of what could have happened, we were so lucky." He reached for her hand, but she moved quickly to the window, looking down through the dusky night into the smoky remains of Courtney's Sports.

Her voice was flat. "I'll tell you why I'm lucky, if that's the word for everything that's happened. I'm lucky that I can still have my old job back at Ladd's. Logan promised it would be waiting for me." She shrugged her slim shoulders. "So I'll be going back. There's nothing left for me here."

"Nothing?" He rose to stand beside her. "Look at me, Courtney. As soon as the fire marshal finishes his investigation for the cause of the fire, you can rebuild any way you wish. You can make it lots better than it was."

"No. As you so aptly put it some time ago, wishes are for dreamers. I haven't enough insurance to cover restocking, let alone rebuilding. I'll be lucky to be able to pay off the bills for what inventory hasn't yet been invoiced. I was going to up the insurance as soon as this first year was under my belt and I knew I could swing it." She leaned her forehead against the cool dark window for just a moment before turning her saddened aqua eyes to his compassionate grey ones. "So much for the best-laid plans. Back to square one, new game." She hesitated. "This probably isn't the best time to offer, but if you could buy my interest I could get a start on some kind of a Capital F future back where I belong. Will you?"

"You belong here in Sister Bay. You love it here. Don't throw that away."

"Please. No sermons. No lawyer-type advice. Just, will you?"

"This is not the time to talk about it. You're upset. Wait until things quiet down."

She shook her head. "I want out. Just answer. Will you? Please?"

He sighed. "Yes. If that's the way you want it."

"I do. Believe me, I do. Thanks. For the coffee, and everything else."

****

Everything else. Those last words of Courtney's three weeks before had come back to haunt Lincoln Spencer a hundred times. He leaned back in his leather chair, looking out over the midtown Chicago area that faced his office window. He rubbed his temples. What had he given her to thank him for? Not what he'd wanted to, certainly. A couple of one-night stands that evidently didn't mean anything to her.

Courtney had left Sister Bay the morning after the fire with a strangely detached look in her dark-circled eyes and nothing more for him than an impersonal handshake. He'd wanted to take her in his arms and kiss her until she looked alive again, but it wasn't the right time for that.

They'd agreed that he would handle the

legalities necessary to relieve her of her interest in the Door County property.

"I'll bring the papers for you to sign," he'd said.

"No. Just mail them. I'll have my signature notarized."

She was adamant. He'd had a pressing legal case that necessitated his immediate return to Chicago and his nearly continuous attendance for twelve-hour days since. Perhaps once that was taken care of he could go up to Sister Bay and get things in order, pick up that copy of Amy's contract with Courtney and take care of the changeover. He sighed. He didn't want the property back; he wanted her on it.

Lincoln presumed that she was already settled in Milwaukee again, resuming the life she'd led before. Probably also resuming her friendship with Logan Andrews. Certainly she wouldn't be alone for long unless she chose to be; she was too attractive for that.

Damn. He'd tried to contact her, but there was no listed phone and he'd hesitated to call during business hours. His thoughts were interrupted by the buzz of his intercom.

"Judge Burns is here to see you, Mr. Spencer."

Lincoln closed his eyes momentarily. At the judge's instruction he had done the legal work to dissolve the Wincar Corporation. The plans for the racecar had been sold to Tracer Bennet at a good price. Perhaps next year it would show up at the Indy under the driver's own sponsorship.

Lincoln sighed. He wasn't ready for another meeting with the bereaved judge. Not right now. But he owed him something, if nothing more than compassion for the loss of his only, overly-pampered daughter. "Send him in."

Breathing heavily, the judge lowered his hulk slowly into the large chair across the desk. "Lincoln."

"Hello, Judge."

There was no cigar in the older man's mouth today. He sucked in a breath that didn't seem to give him enough air, laboriously sucked in another. "Bear with me, will you, Lincoln? This isn't going to be easy for me." His usually assured voice quavered. He seemed to have shrunk in bulk and aged ten years; the usually florid complexion was pasty and his eyes dull, sunk into their sockets.

Spencer waited as the silence lengthened. "Sir?"

"The Sister Bay store...the store that burned...you must be handling it. Have you learned anything about the cause?"

Lincoln shook his head. "Nothing. The investigator seems to think an electrical spark—perhaps from a storm overload on the old wiring may have ignited the gasoline in the storeroom end of the building, though I don't see how. Courtney was always adamant about closing up any gas cans, but perhaps her teenage helper wasn't careful. I don't know. She'd been away and her sister was running the store when her son was lost..." He broke off at the agonized expression on Judge Burn's face. "Why?"

The judge reached into the inside pocket of his jacket and brought out a long slip of paper. He wheezed as he leaned forward and laid it in front of Lincoln.

"What's this?" Link's dark brows met.

The judge cleared his throat and flushed darkly red, looking away from the younger man. "Call it conscience money."

"For what?" Spencer picked up the check and caught his breath in a quick intake as he read the substantial sum on its face. His deep grey eyes met the older man's, questioning. "I thought I made it clear to you that I didn't want your backing, Judge."

"This has nothing to do with whether or not you

choose to run for office."

Spencer frowned. "Then what?"

"It's for...that store." His eyes pools of misery, the judge looked across the desk to Spencer. With difficulty, he cleared his throat and stared at the floor between his heavy thighs. "Georgie started that fire, Lincoln."

"What!" Link dropped both feet flat on the floor and leaned forward.

"I know. I just know she did." The old man's voice was hardly more than a whisper.

"Judge Burns! Are you sure?"

"I'm sure." The Judge dropped his face into the palms of his hands, choking out words between labored sobs. "My baby...my Georgie...gone. And I'm left...it was really my fault, she just misunderstood." He raised his florid face, pleading.

Lincoln Spencer shook his head. "I don't understand."

"She wanted so much, Lincoln. And I promised her. I was so wrong...please take it...to the James woman."

Spencer came around the desk to put his hand on the older man's shoulder. "I'm sorry, Judge..."

The judge looked up, tears running down the folds of his face. "I know. It doesn't matter. Nothing matters any more."

Chapter Twenty-six

Courtney leaned back in her old familiar desk chair and neatly stacked the thick sheaf of invoices she'd been okaying for payment. She sighed deeply and got up to stretch, walking to the window where she could look out over the busy downtown Milwaukee street below. It was the same picture she'd seen so often during the years she'd worked at Ladd's...lots of people, lots of honking cars...only she'd enjoyed it then. Now it seemed so empty.

Nothing is different except me. Longing for a glimpse of the ever-changing, tranquilizing water of Green Bay as she'd watched it so often from her cottage porch, or from the wide front window of the store on the waterfront.

I need to go back, she realized. I didn't think I'd ever want to, after what happened, but I do. Just for a few hours, to be by myself, to gather my thoughts. I left in such a hurry I feel as though I left a part of myself there somewhere, on that little stretch of shore, maybe, or on the rickety steps to the cottage where I watched so many sunsets. I want to find that part of me. It won't take long, maybe just an afternoon. And then I'll be whole again. Then I can move ahead.

In the three weeks she'd been back at Ladd's there had been a lot to catch up on, new people to meet, even some new ways of doing things. But mostly it had been a step back in time. A step that she'd attempted, hoping unsuccessfully that it would erase the past few months from her memory.

For the thousandth time she asked herself why Amy had been so encouraging about opening the store. She must have known what conflict there would be between Courtney and her Great Chicago Lawyer, once he found out that she'd taken over his dream. But, truthfully, did Courtney wish none of it had happened? To never have met and fallen in love with Lincoln Spencer? No matter how it hurt to have it end the way it had? Courtney shook her head and said aloud, "No."

"No?" A masculine voice questioned from her office door, "No, what?"

She whirled, surprised and, she admitted to herself with chagrin, hopeful, but it was only Logan Andrews. Who did she expect? She'd asked Lincoln Spencer to leave her alone, to mail her any papers she had to sign, but nothing had come. Perhaps it wasn't possible to settle anything about the store until the insurance investigation was over. Or was he too desolated, mourning Georgie Burns?

Logan, impeccable as always in shades of grey, lounged against the doorframe. "How can you say no when I haven't even asked you yet?"

She smiled. He really was a dear. Perhaps she was foolish not to encourage him. She knew now that what he'd told her in Chicago was true: there really hadn't been anyone else in his life since she'd left for Door County. "Asked me what?"

"Well, it's a beautiful summer Saturday morning, and you shouldn't even be working, so I thought I'd treat you to a Bloody Mary and a light lunch at that quiet little place around the corner."

"Oh, Logan, thanks. I wasn't saying no to you." Courtney looked out the window again at the bustling weekend morning traffic. "And thanks for the invitation, but—" A decision she didn't even realize she'd made until she spoke it aloud came from nowhere, "I've got some loose ends to wrap up still, and I'm heading north t-to pick up something I forgot when I left Sister Bay so quickly." She smiled. "I'm sorry. Could I get a rain check?"

Logan studied her face for a moment, a resigned expression on his own. "I think I know what you left behind. I hope you find it. Good luck." Before she could ask what he meant, he added, "And yes, the rain check's good any time."

****

Courtney hadn't realized what anticipation she would feel when she turned off the highway with its bumper-to-bumper early August traffic and drove toward the cool woods along the Green Bay shore. What I left behind, she thought as she braked to a stop on the gravel drive under sighing white pines, was my heart and soul. How I've missed this.

She crossed her bare arms over the steering wheel and drank in the sight of the softly lapping water she could see over the roof of her— correction—what *had* been her cottage. The opposite shore was only a suggestion in the haze that shimmered off the blue-grey surface. From up here, she couldn't see the blackened remains of Courtney's Sports. She didn't want to, not just yet. She just wanted to be here alone, let the quiet soothe her.

After a moment, she realized how warm it was in her car. Though her hair was caught back in a blue ribbon to match her linen slacks, its heavy length lay like a blanket on her moist neck.

I'd better do what I came for, she thought, getting out of the car. Gather my thoughts. She pulled her shoulder bag from the front seat, glad she hadn't forgotten to toss in her new blue bikini. Her faithful red one had burned with the store.

One last swim. One last look. For what, she wasn't really sure. She just knew she had to close this chapter, turn this page with finality before she could get on with living, wherever or whatever that

213

would prove to be.

Courtney opened her cottage door with the key that was still hidden over the sill. She'd have to remember to mail that to Lincoln when she sent back the signed papers.

The cottage smelled musty and seemed smaller and darker than she remembered. She felt ghosts hovering in it, and hurried to slip out of her slacks and blouse and into her scanty bikini. She caught up a beach towel and let the screen door slam shut behind her as she walked down the path between the cottages to the private little stretch of pebbled beach a half-block down from the dock. Later, she would go back to the ruins of the store, look over the destruction and lay away her dreams. Right now all she wanted was to stretch out in the sun and sort things out.

She spread her towel and lay face down on it, feeling oddly misplaced, more psychologically empty than physically tired. Since she'd been back at Ladd's her most strenuous moves had been to get herself a cup of coffee. She stretched and smiled ruefully. Who would have thought she'd miss the challenge of starting a reluctant boat motor, or helping a novice fisherman choose the right angling equipment?

Her thoughts went back over the summer, and she smiled for real as she thought of Lisbet's coming wedding to Jerry, who had made the momentous decision to stop race driving and go into teaching. "Life is too precious now," he'd said, one arm around a radiant Lisbet, the other protectively circling Andy's shoulders. Perfect for them, for dear little Andy. He'd recovered from their damp imprisonment with no ill effects, and he and Lisbet were still at their cottage up the way; she'd stop to see them before driving back to Milwaukee later.

Courtney wiggled into a more comfortable

position and closed her eyes, letting scenes from the summer play through her mind. Putting the store together...meeting Lincoln Spencer on this same strip of shoreline...the fish boil...Andy's water skiing triumph...the island...the magic night in Chicago. She relived the tumultuous plane ride when she had realized how much she loved Link...the storm, the hours in the dark hillside cave...the embarrassing scene in front of Spencer's fireplace...and poor Georgie Burns.

A splash startled her, and she rolled over to stare up at the handsome heavy-browed, swim-suited man who'd risen from the Bay and now stood between her and the afternoon sun.

"Hello." The familiar voice was low and husky. "Haven't we played this scene before?"

Courtney's body flooded with warmth. "Oh! I didn't know you were here! There was no car in your drive—" She looked away, reaching back for her towel. "I'm sorry. Now I really am trespassing..." She began to rise, but his lean hand on her shoulder held her back as he dropped down beside her. "Courtney."

She didn't look at him. "I'll go." What else could she say? Embarrassing, unwanted tears suddenly flooded her eyes. "I-I just wanted—"

"Wanted what?" He cupped her chin in his hand, forcing her to look up.

"I-I don't know. I left so suddenly that part of me is still here, I think." She was babbling but she had to explain. She wanted to throw herself into his arms against the water-sparkled mat on his chest. His rebelliously waving hair was darkly wet as it had been on that day of their first meeting. At least this time she was decently covered. "I-I needed to be here for just a little while. I don't seem to fit back in the city—"

"No. You don't fit there. Not any more." His strong hand lightly brushed a strand of honey-blond hair from her sun-warmed shoulder. "Amy knew it, and I know it. Everyone seems to know it but you." His eyes were deep grey pools, pulling her in. "I've been waiting since yesterday. I knew you had to come."

"You knew?"

"To come after your heart...but you'll have to take mine instead."

She caught her breath. "What did you say?"

"You gave me yours that night on the island." At her confused look, he said, "Remember when I asked if you meant what you said when you were falling asleep?"

"I remember your asking." She looked away.

"For the rest of your life, were your exact words."

Her memory was stirred by his recounting of her love-sated, sleep-filled words. She put up her chin. "I wasn't accountable. You seduced me wickedly. And if I remember our conversation in the morning, you said you wouldn't hold me to it."

"I lied. Come here." He pulled her into his arms, his lips tender, claiming hers tentatively at first, then more forcefully as he felt her body respond. "I love you, Courtney James." His hands slid down her arms to her waist, bringing her against him as he lay down and pulled her on top of him. "I've loved you from the first minute I saw you here, so vulnerable, so fiercely independent. Say you love me, too. Now, when you're awake!" His husky words were a moan against her neck as his lips trailed down to the mound of her breast. "Say it, Courtney! I can't, I won't wait any longer!"

She closed her eyes, her body melting against his as though she would become part of him, her voice soft as the waves lapping against the pebbled shore. "I do. Oh, Link, I do. I think I always have."

His hand stroked her waist, caressed her hip

and moved up to cup her breast, thumbing her nipple to an aroused peak through the fragile material of her suit as his tongue explored the sweetness of her willing mouth for aching moments before she pushed against his chest and struggled to sit up. Her breath came in short little catches and his arms were pulling her to him again as she said into his shoulder, "What do you mean, Amy knew? I don't understand."

"There's a lot you don't understand, yet." He rolled her body gently onto her back and leaned over her. The sun above him lit a damp halo around his dark head. "After you left, when I was looking for your contract, I found a letter to me, about you. Amy knew she wasn't well. She hoped—" he ran his hand teasingly down Courtney's blushed cheek, "—and planned, that you and I would find our futures here. Together."

"Miss Amy planned...you and I?" It was hard to concentrate on what he was saying while his lips rained soft kisses on her face, her eyes.

"Those impossible eyes. I couldn't get them out of my mind. God, Courtney, I've missed you." His chuckle was low and sensuous. "Why do you think she talked you into starting the store I'd always meant to open? My Aunt Amy wasn't one to leave anything to chance." His lips traced a pattern of fire down Courtney's throat to the mounds of her breasts. "Do you like this?"

"Stop! I can't think!"

"I don't want you to think. I want you to feel."

"But what about..." she held him away with her hands against his chest. "Georgie was so obvious about owning you."

"Poor little Georgie." His eyes were thoughtful as with one finger he retraced the line of Courtney's cheek, down her throat to the cleavage between her breasts. "I did think I loved her once a very long time ago." He looked up into the quiet pines for a moment. "But I grew up." He smiled then and kissed the tip of her nose. "By the way, I have a present for you. From the judge."

"Judge Burns?" Courtney struggled to sit up but the strong arms on either side of her held her captive. "Georgie's father?"

"It's a long story. I'll tell you all about it, and about you...and me...and the future of Courtney's Sports." He nuzzled the soft spot under her right ear, "And about a certain lawyer who's moving his practice to Sister Bay." He pulled back to smile tenderly into her eyes. "It might take a while. Do you have enough time to listen?"

She looked up at him, her eyes a brilliant reflection of the August sky, her mouth soft with longing for his love. "Time? Oh, yes...only the rest of my life."

Her voice was stilled by his lips as his dark head bent over her light one while the afternoon sun moved slowly across the sky above Sister Bay.

Thank you for purchasing this Wild Rose Press publication. For other wonderful stories of romance, please visit our on-line bookstore at www.thewildrosepress.com.

For questions or more information contact us at info@thewildrosepress.com.

The Wild Rose Press
www.TheWildRosePress.com